David McRobbie

See How They Run

PUFFIN BOOKS

PUFFIN BOOKS

Published by the Penguin Group
Penguin Books Ltd, 27 Wrights Lane, London W8 5TZ, England
Penguin Putnam Inc., 375 Hudson Street, New York, New York 10014, USA
Penguin Books Australia Ltd, Ringwood, Victoria, Australia
Penguin Books Canada Ltd, 10 Alcorn Avenue, Toronto, Ontario, Canada M4V 3B2
Penguin Books (NZ) Ltd, Private Bag 102902, NSMC, Auckland, New Zealand

On the worldwide web at: www.penguin.com

Penguin Books Ltd, Registered Offices: Harmondsworth, Middlesex, England

First published in Australia by Penguin Books Australia Ltd 1996
Published in Puffin Books 1996
3 5 7 9 10 8 6 4

Film and television tie-in edition first published 1999

Copyright © David McRobbie, 1996
All rights reserved

Filmset in

Made and printed in England by Clays Ltd, St Ives plc

British Library Cataloguing in Publication Data
A CIP catalogue record for this book is available from the British Library

ISBN 0-141-30333-6

1

Maybe if I hadn't dawdled on the way home from school, it mightn't have been so bad. Mum was always going on at me about dawdling and, on this particular afternoon, if I hadn't wasted time, the story might have had an easier beginning. For me it was the end of an ordinary school day in Timperley, just south of Manchester, a place we were never to see again.

It was a simple thing that held me up: I'd gone to a friend's house. Her name was Sandra. It still is, I suppose. As it happened, she was my best friend, and we had known each other since early primary school days, reaching our fifteenth years together. Sandra's house was three streets from ours, so I wasn't far away. And we were only listening to a CD that Sandra had been given for her birthday. Not all of it, there wasn't time. We just spotted through the different tracks, making comments as we went – 'Yeah, terrific', things like that – until it was time to go.

'Mum'll create,' I remember saying to Sandra, as I looked at my watch. She giggled. Our mums were always creating. So I waved to Sandra and said ta-ra, or something light and commonplace. See-you-in-the-morning, that sort of thing. If I'd known what was waiting for me at home, I'd definitely have made the parting from Sandra a lot more significant, more heart-felt. Fervent! Yes, that's the word. There would have been tears, hugs and promises never to forget each other.

We'd never see each other again, and it would be a long time before poor Sandra would learn the reason. And she wouldn't hear it from me.

When I reached home, parked in front of our house were two dark cars with tinted windows – Granadas, identical except for their registration numbers. I saw them as soon as I turned the corner into Stretton Road, but because of those windows it was impossible to see if anyone was inside. I didn't like to stare, but somehow they were ominous looking. I had a feeling they were to do with us. I let the garden gate swing shut behind me and took the Yale key out of my schoolbag. Two lovely little familiar, homely things: the noise the gate made as it squeaked to a close behind me, then being able to tell by feel alone which key was which. They too were to be last-time things. As I walked up the path to the front door I could hear Mum's voice.

'Oh, where can she be? It's just not like Emma to be so late.'

'Come on, Lil.' That was Dad's big rumble of a voice. 'It's only been half an hour. Maybe she's been held back in class. Or it's sports club, or an assignment, anything.' It was strange that Dad should be home from the office this early in the afternoon. By now I'd got the key out of my bag. Something was definitely up. Nicola, my younger sister, suddenly bobbed up at the front window and saw me.

'She's here,' I heard her announce. 'Emma's home.' Before I could fit the key into the deadlock, the door opened, and Mum was there, with a huge look of relief on her face. She almost dragged me over the threshold.

'Where have you been, Emma? All this time, where have you *been*?'

'Mum, I just stopped off – ' But then this strange woman came from the living room, closed the front door behind us, and took over.

'Emma, your mother's packed a bag for you.'

'Packed a bag? For me? Why?'

'We ought to go now, Mrs Cassidy.' A tall man suddenly appeared. 'All packed? All set?' He glanced around.

'But – ' I started to say, looking from one to the other of these strangers. Who were they? What was going on? There was another man in the living room, half a head shorter than the first, with a bushy moustache that spread across his cheeks. Three of them in all, but they looked friendly enough – sympathetic, almost kind – so I wasn't worried by their sudden appearance, nor threatened by them, just mystified. I had a thousand questions.

'Later, Em,' Dad said. 'I'll explain on the way.'

'On the way where?' But no one answered. At that moment, Barney, our dog, came bustling in from the back garden with a stick in his mouth, ready for the game we usually played when I came home from school.

3

Seeing him, Mum suddenly broke down in tears.

'Oh, what about the dog? What about Barney?'

'Our people'll fix him,' the man with the moustache assured Mum. 'We've done it often enough. Feed, water, the lot. He'll be all right. Good home, you know.' He knelt and offered his fingers to Barney and made kissing noises. 'Here, boy. Come on, boy. You'll be fine, eh?' Barney growled, and backed away from the stranger.

Dad went to Mum, offering a consoling hand, but she brushed him away. He stood awkwardly, trying to pretend he'd been going to do something else with that hand. He was hurt.

'I'll take the lead car,' the tall man said, as he opened the front door. 'Mrs Cassidy, you come with me and, um – ' He looked directly at me.

'Emma.' Flatly I supplied my name.

'Yes, Emma. Mr Cassidy and Nicola can follow in the second car.'

It was like some sort of dream. Numb and confused, I just went where they put me, did what they said. They were quick about it, as if they'd done this sort of thing before. After we were all outside on the garden path, the woman locked our front door then dropped the keys into *her* pocket. It seemed so *final*. They were our keys, this was our home, yet now she seemed to have possession of it.

'A security firm will be checking the place,' the woman said. 'We always use them.'

Mum and I got into the back of the first car, while the woman took the front passenger seat. The tall man drove but the woman seemed to be in charge. I could see Dad and Nicola getting into the second Granada, which took off after us.

Were they bailiffs? Was this an eviction? I knew Dad had one or two troubles at work but I had never imagined it was this bad. Had we somehow lost ownership of our house?

We drove away, moving fast, both cars keeping close together. It was early November, and already growing dark at this time in the afternoon, so there were no people in their front gardens to watch us go. A few pedestrians were in the street, but only one or two kids on bikes paused to stare at the identical dark-windowed cars hurrying past. We stopped at the traffic lights at the end of our street, ready to turn into the main road.

The car with Mum and me in it took the left lane, and the one with Dad and Nicola drew alongside, ready to turn right. The tinted windows allowed me to see out, but not into the car next to us. I wanted very much to make contact with my father, or Nicola: any kind of communication that would help make sense of this. The lights changed to green and we moved off in different directions.

'But – ' I said. 'Where are they taking Dad? And Nicola?'

'It's okay, Emma.' The woman turned around in her seat to reassure me. 'They're just going by a different route. You'll see them again soon enough.' Mum looked out of her window then leaned forward trying to catch sight of the other car, but it was already lost in the traffic. She sighed deeply and settled back to stare at her fingers, as if she didn't want to catch my eye.

'Mum.' I dropped my voice to a whisper. 'What's this about?' Mum sort of gnawed her lip, the way she did when there were big decisions to be made. She had difficulty getting the sentence out.

'Your dad's got himself into a bit of – ' Mum paused, choosing the next word. 'Trouble.'

'Dad?' My eyes were wide. 'Dad? In trouble?'

How could someone like my dad be in trouble? It wasn't the sort of thing you'd expect of him. He's a big, open, easygoing Australian. He came over from Brisbane with qualifications in accountancy, intending to study economics – which is how he met Mum, who was reading English Literature at the University of Manchester.

Nicola and I loved to hear Mum and Dad give their different versions of how they met. Dad said that Mum swept him off his feet and wouldn't take no for an answer, while Mum always claimed it wasn't like that at all. Mum had been working at a library table, with books all around her, when Dad came and sat opposite her and tried to find enough space for his own books. Mum maintained that she was so deeply immersed in her work she didn't even notice Dad, whereas Dad said that Mum hogged all the space deliberately, knowing full well that this tall, handsome young man would have to say something.

Anyway, whatever the truth of it, they married. Dad gave up his studies and found accountancy work in the city. Mum, who had graduated by then, worked for a publisher until she became pregnant with me. So my parents settled down, and then two years later Nicola was born. What with Mum not wanting to travel with young children, and Dad doing really lucrative work with an accounting firm in Manchester, specialising in company takeovers and investments, somehow Dad just gave up the idea of going back to Brisbane, though he'd often joke about not being Australian any more.

'Now I've picked up all these Pommy habits, they won't let me back in,' he used to say, then he'd put on a broad Aussie accent. 'Yair, had to hand in me slouch hat with little corks round it, me bottle-opener and didgeridoo, the lot. Fair dinkum. Makes yer spit.'

While Dad often made wisecracks about his origins, he always promised that one day the four of us would visit Australia, maybe even stay for a while. But Nicola and I regarded ourselves as English through and through. Sometimes, just for a laugh, we'd put on broad Manchester accents and say things like 'oop' or 'coom'.

'Coom on, Nicola,' I called upstairs one Saturday morning. We had netball to go to. 'Time to get oop!'

'Emma, I'm coomin',' Nicola answered. Dad heard us from the bathroom where he was shaving, and took the bait.

'Oop and coom?' Then he imitated Ms Sangster, my English teacher, who was always on the look-out for what she called careless speech. 'Now girls,' Dad said in a high-pitched, scolding tone. 'Can't allow slipshod diction, can we?'

In summer, when it was cricket season, we used to have arguments about test matches because Nicola and I supported England while Dad was all for Australia. Mum kept right out of these debates.

'It's only a game,' she once said. 'A lot of silly men hawking and spitting, running about hugging each other. Not to mention the way they polish the ball.' The three of us pretended to be deeply shocked. We'd shake our heads and heave a huge sigh.

'Only a game?' Dad whistled in disbelief. 'Don't ever say a thing like that outside these four walls, will you Lil?'

A man like that – what kind of trouble could he be in?

It was quite dark now. The car was in the country, heading somewhere, but our driver was avoiding the motorway and the main routes, sticking to the B-roads. From the signs that flashed up in our headlights, I recognised places we had visited as kids, when Dad or Mum used to take us for drives in Daimler, which was back there in the garage beside the house. They had been special days, because Dad would only take Daimler out occasionally. Right from the start, Nicola and I had started calling the car 'Daimler', not 'the Daimler', because we decided it was more swish or something – at least I think that's how the name came about. Dad mainly used a company car, a BMW – or the Beamer, as

Nicola called it – while Mum drove a silver-grey Honda.

Rain had started. It wasn't quite heavy enough for the windscreen-wipers to be on all the time, so every now and then they'd make a monotonous swipe-swipe, then stop.

'Where are we going?' I said, addressing nobody in particular. 'Somebody can at least tell me that.' No one had spoken for the last twenty-five minutes. It was the woman in the front seat who answered.

'Just taking you to a place where you'll stay for the night.'

'But why do we need to stay for the night? What's going on anyway?'

'Look, I'm sorry, Emma.' This time the woman turned right around to face me. She held out a hand and squeezed mine. 'It's best we don't say too much, for now. But try not to worry.'

'What about Dad?' I spoke to Mum, who sat beside me, nursing her own thoughts. 'Tell me.'

'He's all right,' she answered, putting a slight emphasis on the 'he's', as if Dad was somehow in the wrong. Mum was more-or-less saying he'd caused all this. Whatever it was. The windscreen-wipers went into their routine again. That's all the explanation I was going to be given. Swipe-swipe. Brush me aside. I folded my arms and looked out of the window.

It was strange, I felt, that Mum didn't explain things to me. We'd always been able to talk openly together, talks

9

where I could share my feelings with her, things I'd never say to anyone else. Then Mum would sit me down and we'd talk it through. When I was smaller, they were simple schoolgirl concerns.

'Now, Emma,' Mum would say. 'Are you sure you're not being just a little bit uncharitable?'

'Me, uncharitable? Of course not.' I'd come home complaining because another girl, Flora, had had her painting accepted to go on display for parents' day at school.

'Well, maybe you're a bit jealous.'

'I'm not jealous.'

'Well, all of the other girls didn't have their paintings chosen. What are they saying?'

'Um – they're not saying much. But their paintings aren't as good as mine.'

'Or as good as Flora's?'

'Well, no.'

'So Flora's painting is pretty good?'

'Well, yes.'

'As good as yours?'

'Yes.'

'Not much to choose between them?'

'No.'

And we'd go on like that until I calmed down. When I grew older, and nearly as tall as Mum, there came other concerns, about how I looked and what I felt, and always Mum would listen calmly, looking at me with her steady grey eyes, never laughing at me or making me feel silly for saying what I'd said. So as we sat silently in that car,

I wanted my mother to do as she'd always done, in that lovely, patient way, and explain what was happening.

By now we were on one of the motorways that spread out from Manchester, the M56, which even at this time of night was crowded with cars and lorries, all going west. So that, at least, was some glimmer of information.

Dad was honest; he was fair and even-handed. Whenever he and Mum gave one of us something big – like the time they paid for riding lessons for Nicola, or the time I took up the guitar – Dad used to go into what he called the scales-of-justice routine.

'Oh dear,' he'd say. 'Nicola's having riding lessons.' Then he'd hold his arms out to the sides and let his hands drop down, as if he had suddenly become a set of scales. One arm would drop as the other came up. This pantomime was to represent the scales being out of balance, in Nicola's favour. 'So what can we do to even things up?'

'Dad,' I protested. 'Aren't we getting a bit old for this? Nicola can have her riding lessons. I don't mind.' He'd ignore me.

'Oh dear, it's a poser. What can we do?' Then he'd reach into his jacket pocket and bring out a bar of chocolate or some such thing, and hold out his arm again. Slowly the scales would come back into balance. 'There you are, Em. All square now.' He'd give me the chocolate or whatever. Always it was something ridiculously small, a bag of M & M's or some such, Dad's joke being that this tiny thing was equal in value to riding lessons.

'Oh thanks, Dad,' I'd say gravely, and of course we'd have to share the gift around.

In the back of the car, I smiled to myself as I remembered such silly incidents – but fair and even-handed in everything he did, that was my dad.

Things went bad for a while. The accounting practice he'd been with for years folded suddenly. Then Dad joined with a friend, Alec Cowan, to start their own consultancy. It took some months to build up a client list. Dad threw himself into the new practice, in his usual manner, but you could tell he was having trouble. His jokey ways disappeared, he'd work longer hours, leaving the house in the morning before Nicola and I were up, that sort of thing. He'd not come back till late at night.

With the collapse of the previous accounting practice, the BMW had gone so Dad travelled to work on an orange GM bus each morning. He grew worried and preoccupied, and that went on for weeks, with Mum supporting him – us too of course – financially and in other ways. My mother worked from home, editing a series of biographies of writers from the north of England. During most of this time, Mum's was the only money that came in.

We left the motorway at a place called Sworton Heath, then for a while we were on a narrow B-road. Signs flickered past but, because of the raindrops that rolled diagonally down the window-glass, they might as well have been in Chinese. Apart from that there was little to see in the countryside around, except the odd light. Progress was slow and cars followed us. Up ahead I saw a blue flashing light, then a reflective sign which said POLICE – STOP. Our driver slowed to a halt and his electric window whined down. I shivered in the sudden draught of cold air that drifted into the car. A rain-drenched policeman leaned down at the open window and nodded.

'I'll give you two minutes,' he said. 'That enough time for you?'

'Yep, that'll do,' our driver agreed, then let the car roll forward as his window whined up again. I looked back. The policeman had already held up the line of cars behind us. He was leaning in the window of the first vehicle, talking to the driver, when we turned a corner.

As we drove, the countryside was flat and featureless. I searched for some kind of landmark, or a road sign to show where we were, but there was nothing. Then we came to a roundabout, at which the road ahead of us divided into three directions.

'Straight on,' the woman instructed the driver, who nodded. She seemed to be consulting some sort of route written in a notepad she kept on her knee, using the light from the glove box to see what she was reading. In seconds we had joined other traffic and passed through a long, brightly lit tunnel. We came out to see a sign which directed us to various towns, none of which I now remember.

'I could do this for a living,' the driver joked.

'So what's my father done?' I asked the woman.

'You'll know tonight, Emma,' she answered. 'Your father will explain.'

'Are you the police?'

'Yes.' The woman had a small laugh in her voice. 'We're the good guys.' I turned to look out of the back window of the car. There was nothing behind us.

For Dad and Alec Cowan, it finally looked as if things were improving. He didn't need to announce it. We could tell by the way he changed again – back to the old Dad we used to know. It was as if he'd stepped out of a deep shadow into the light. The partnership was working out at last.

I could tell he'd turned the corner when I went to school with him one cold morning. Nicola, who usually left for school later, went a different direction with Mum in the Honda, while Dad and I went on the bus. I did suggest we take Daimler, but Dad wouldn't hear of it. 'Wash your mouth out, Emma!' he protested. 'Daimler's not your everyday car.'

As we walked together down Stretton Road, I could sense the spring in my father's step, which I didn't really welcome at the time. Honestly, when you've been up late, studying till your eyes hurt and your head swims, the last thing you want is a cheerful father cracking jokes. To match my mood, morose was what I required. Before we'd got more than a dozen paces away from our front garden gate, Dad opened the attack. 'Shoulders back,

Emma. Head up. Walk tall. That's my girl.'

'Oh, come on, Dad. I'll slouch if I want to.'

'You walk as if you've got a leg on each corner.' Dad hunched his shoulders forward and plodded along beside me, looking grim, as if we'd turned into a matched pair, big and little. Then he straightened up and became himself again. 'Emma, you should place one foot exactly behind the other and move fluently. Ladies should glide.'

'Ladies?' I snorted. 'Not these days.'

'Well, women then. Go on, try it, Em. Swing along, walk tall. Serene and graceful. They're the watchwords.' He demonstrated how I should walk, swaying his hips and looking ridiculous.

'Like this, Father?' I asked sweetly.

'That's the way, Em, only don't dawdle, or we'll miss the bus.'

'Can't glide *and* hurry,' I protested. So I gave up the ladylike serenity of movement and ran to keep pace beside him.

'Work on it in your own time,' Dad advised me. 'Or when you're out with your mum. You can do it together. And your little sister.'

'Somebody's in a good mood,' I said.

'Business is looking up, Em.' We walked on until we reached the bus-stop where some people were waiting, huddled and stamping their feet against the cold. 'Six more months of this and we might manage that trip to Australia. How about that?'

'Great, Dad.' I was in rapture at the idea. 'The Opera

15

House, Sydney Harbour, the Barrier Reef.'

'It's summer there.' Dad sniffed the cold, English morning air. 'Oh, can't you smell the beaches, the sun-burned country, the wind off the sea, the carefree days and balmy nights?' He sighed appreciatively, which made people in the queue look at him strangely.

And he was in trouble?

Now we'd got on to an A-road, where the car moved fast in the centre lane. After a few minutes we branched off at a sign which directed us to Knutsford. I couldn't believe it! In darkness and rain we'd driven all around the southern outskirts of Manchester, only to end up ten or twelve kilometres from home. From the way the driver kept ducking his head forward, looking for signs and landmarks, I could tell this was where we were to stop. I'd often been to Knutsford on our family outings in Daimler. Dad would drive us majestically through the narrow streets while Mum, Nicola and I admired the old black-and-white houses and shops.

'Daimler's just right for a visit to Knutsford,' Dad had once said. 'Both British to the bootstraps.' On another occasion, I went there on an excursion with my English class, which was Ms Sangster's idea.

'Girls, you can't go to school near Knutsford and not pay your respects,' she had explained to us. 'It was where Mrs Gaskell spent her early years.'

'Yes, Miss,' we chorused. We already knew about the connection between Mrs Gaskell, Knutsford and her famous novel *Cranford*, and about Ms Sangster's particular interest in that Victorian author. We grew up on Knutsford lore, knowing for example that the town got its name from King Canute, originally being called Canutesford, and that in the parish church grounds is the grave of the man whose trumpet sounded the order to begin the Charge of the Light Brigade.

Before long we slowed, then drove into the car park of a fairly modern hotel. Knutsford Inn, I read on a swinging sign, which stood by the roadside, showing a picture of an old-fashioned stagecoach.

'This is it,' said the policewoman in the front seat.

'All present and correct,' the driver added. Ahead of us, the other Granada was already parked near the front entrance – but there was no sign of Dad or Nicola. Our driver switched off the lights and the engine. 'You folks go in, I'll bring the bags,' he said as he got out. After the warmth of the car it was cold in the car park. I shivered and the woman went around to help Mum.

Inside the hotel foyer it was cheerful enough, but it wasn't really an old-fashioned place. They had just decorated it that way for the tourist trade – polished horse brasses, copper warming-pans, bellows, hunting prints with impossibly elongated horses, dark, ancient-looking wooden beams with artificially aged wrought iron, that sort of thing – but nothing you could call a genuine antique. In a room off the main entrance, a large wood fire burned in a stone fireplace. Dad came to greet us.

'We've got two rooms,' he said. 'You girls are in together.' He dithered, then went to help the man who was coming in with our bags. Dad had something else on his mind. 'Um,' he began when he came back, looking around to make sure he wasn't being overheard. 'We're registered here as the Morton family.'

'Who are they?' I said.

'They're us, Em.' Dad kept his voice low. 'So if anyone asks, tell them you're Emma Morton.'

2

As a family, we'd often stayed in hotels, going away for holidays or weekends during better financial times, but those events were nothing like this. We didn't belong in the Knutsford Inn. We should have been safely, warmly at home, doing evening things as thousands of other people were doing right at that moment. In the hotel foyer all the adults, Mum, Dad and the police, went into a planning huddle, leaving Nicola and me to our own thoughts. By now we were caught up in how critical our situation must be. The hole-in-the-wall, cloak-and-dagger stuff had had its effect on us and we'd both worked out it had to be serious, whatever it was, but no one took the time to tell us *what* it was.

In all our other hotel stays and stopovers, we'd always known we'd go back home to our own things. Once we were driving north in the Lake District when the BMW had not one, but two, punctures, so we had to stay in a boarding house till the garage sent for a new tyre. Well, the hotel was like something out of *Fawlty Towers*. Just before we arrived, the manager had been in a fight with his wife, who'd hit him and opened a cut above his eye. Later, in the dining room, he tried to maintain his dignity, carry on chatty conversations and so on, while we did our best to keep straight faces.

We were doing pretty well until another guest, who was obviously a permanent fixture in the place, leaned over and whispered to Dad, 'Happens all the time, you know. These two, at it like cat and dog they are. Violence, you never saw the like.' Then the guest drew in a long breath, closed his eyes and shook his head.

Nicola had just taken a mouthful of something from her plate, and she began to choke. We all jumped up, alternatively giggling and thumping her on the back, then the manager came into the dining room and saw us. He just slumped and started to cry, dabbing his eyes with a bloody handkerchief.

It was awful.

But in the busy foyer of Knutsford Inn there was to be no giggling between Nicola and me. Already we had a sense that in the morning we wouldn't be going back home. The whole situation was so unusual, so dreamlike. We stood there numbly, with me feeling right out of place in my school uniform, while other guests came and went, dressed for dinner. There was some kind of function on that night. Before escorting his wife into the dining room, a man raised an eyebrow at me – ordinary little me in my school outfit, trying not to stand out like some kind of freak.

'Were you home when the police came, Nicola?'

'Only just.' She nodded.

'Well, what did they say? The police.'

'Nothing much,' Nicola told me. 'Dad was already there and Mum had our bags packed. The big worry was you, Emma, why you were late – '

'I've been late home before,' I said defensively.

Dad suddenly cut short our discussion by putting a hand on each of our shoulders. 'It's best we get out of the foyer, girls. Let's go up to your room.' He shepherded us towards the stairs. 'We'll eat there. Room service, eh?'

'Dad,' I hissed. 'Tell me.'

'Tell me too,' Nicola added.

'Yep,' he agreed, then smiled and nodded to another guest who was coming downstairs for dinner. He waited until we were in the wide, carpeted corridor of the upper floor before speaking again. 'The fact is, darlings, we're on the run.'

Our room was modern and looked quite comfortable. Unlike the imitation Olde-Worlde appearance of downstairs, the bedroom was functional, with yellow wood furniture and so on. There was a television set, tea-making things, and two single beds with a small table between them, on which was a telephone. There was also a bathroom and toilet. The two bags that Mum had packed were already there, and someone had drawn the curtains and turned down the beds.

'On the run?' I said. 'What, like criminals?'

'We've done nothing wrong,' Dad assured me, then amended his statement. '*I've* done nothing wrong.' At that moment, there came a tiny knock at the door and Dad opened it to allow Mum into the room.

'Have you told the girls, Don?'

'About to,' Dad said. 'But it's better if you're here too, Lil.' Nicola and I sat on our beds while Mum took one of the chairs. Dad stood up.

'I did some work for a man – '

'A criminal?' I cut Dad off.

'A good description,' Mum agreed, with a sudden note of anger in her voice. Dad wasn't enjoying this.

'It's better that you girls don't know too many details,' he went on. 'What I can say is this man had criminal connections – drugs mainly – but I didn't know that. I only saw his respectable face, his office just off Fountain Street, a nice house in Heaton Park with a three-car garage, his charming wife and three teenage kids at private schools.' He sighed. 'So without going into too many technicalities, I did some of this work for him until the police moved in.'

'It was money laundering,' Mum explained. 'Making dirty money clean.'

'When criminals make money illegally,' Dad went on, 'it's usually in the form of cash, so they either have to hide it or channel it into investments and so on – '

'His drug money?' Nicola asked.

'Mainly.' Dad nodded. 'Anyway, for the last couple of months, I have been – ' He paused. ' – concerned about the way things were developing, so I tried to break off my association with this man. But, only two days ago, he was arrested. The police are still investigating, trying to unravel the money trail. It's big. Millions of pounds, a lot of it offshore, the Bahamas, safe havens. That's where Alec and I were involved.' Again Dad paused. 'Alec was in deeper than I was. He had more of an idea what was going on.'

'But you're not a crook,' Nicola said.

'No, your father's only a witness,' Mum rushed to assure us. 'Only a witness.'

'So you'll have to give evidence, Dad?' I asked.

'That's about it,' he agreed. 'Which is why we're on the run – for our safety.'

'If he's been arrested, why do we need to hide?' Nicola protested. 'Why are we on the run?'

'That's how it works,' Dad explained, but Nicola still wasn't satisfied.

'But if the criminal's in jail – '

'Custody,' Dad corrected her. Still Nicola wasn't to be put off.

'Custody, jail, whatever. If he's in jail then why aren't we safe?'

'He has friends, Nicola,' Mum explained. She paused, looking bleakly at the television set. 'There's no nice way to say this. He just doesn't want your father to give evidence against him.'

'What a gorgon,' Nicola said softly then turned away. 'An ugly, slimy, snakes-for-hair gorgon.' Gorgon was her current insult, the worst slur she could think of. A week later it would be something else. Mum put both hands

23

on Nicola's shoulder and leaned over, brushing her cheek against Nicola's hair.

'Shh, darling,' I heard Mum say, which made me want consolation from my mother too.

'Couldn't Dad just say no, he won't do it?' I appealed to Mum's back, then turned to face Dad. 'I mean, if you refuse, Dad – if you just refuse then that's it, isn't it?'

'Not really, Emma.' Dad spoke gently. Then it was his turn to be bleak. 'You see, I know too much about his finances and his affairs, which makes me a threat. And as long as I continue to endanger him, he can never rest.'

After that, there was a long silence while all sorts of thoughts chased each other through my mind. With millions of pounds at stake, with a long jail sentence in front of you, and only one man holding the key, what do you do? Simple. You remove that one man. I bit my lip so hard I tasted blood.

My father was now a protected witness. And we were too, of course, protected dependents, because if the particular gorgon can't get at the witness, then the family will do just as well.

I'd read an article in the *Manchester Evening News* about witness protection schemes. These days, big cities like ours were becoming famous for it. Someone commits a crime and is arrested. The police produce a witness, but the only way they can get the witness to speak out in court is to give complete protection, which sometimes means the witness has to assume a new identity and take his or her family to live in a completely different part of Britain.

It's always in the papers about how witnesses are intimidated into keeping quiet, so that the criminal walks free, smiling his triumph from the steps of the Criminal Court, giving the police the finger as he leaves with his friends. It used to make me angry, but never in my worst dreams did I think it would touch us. That sort of thing always seemed to affect people who lived in places where the crimes were punch-ups, violence, robberies and the like – nothing to do with us in safe, semi-detached Timperley.

There was another light tap on the door and Dad opened it. The policewoman was outside. Dad ushered her in.

'How's it going?' she asked.

'Okay,' Nicola shrugged and broke away from Mum, putting on a brave face for the policewoman. 'Hard to take in, though.'

'Doesn't get easier,' the policewoman agreed. 'Food's on its way up. There's a couple of our people in Room 12, just for the night. It's along the hall on the left. Can you be ready to move by seven-thirty in the morning?'

'Yes.' Dad spoke for all of us.

'Move where?' Mum said.

The policewoman hesitated then smiled.

'A safe house. I'm not quite sure. The fewer who know the better, eh?' She smiled again. Tomorrow she'd be home in her own place with her familiar things and faces around her. It was just a job. 'Right. Seven-thirty then?' The policewoman nodded, and backed out into the hall just as the room-service waiter wheeled in our dinners on a little trolley. He was Irish and cheerily full of banter. They were like actors, I thought, coming in and going out, first the tragedy then the comedy.

'Here we are now.' The Irish waiter tried to raise a laugh. 'I hope some of ye's has royal blood in yer veins for this here's a feast for a king.' But none of us had the mood to match his.

After he'd gone, we all stood there, unwilling to move towards the trolley. It was Nicola who made the first observation.

'Maybe the Gorgon's poisoned the food.'

I've never been able to sleep properly in hotels and strange beds. It was worse that night in the Knutsford Inn because there were all of these crushing thoughts to grapple with. It was still early, about nine o'clock, and neither of us felt like watching television. Mum and Dad had gone to their room – reluctantly on Mum's part, but Nicola and I insisted she go. After all, Dad needed her too. I kept having guilty feelings that I should have done my homework, but my schoolbag was back in the living room at home where I'd dropped it.

Nicola's poison remark hadn't been completely out-rageous and tasteless, and that's not a pun either. For a while, we'd all sat staring at the trolley with its plates and knives, napkins and warm bread rolls.

'Na. Can't be.' Dad broke the silence by lifting the lid

of the soup tureen. He sniffed the contents. 'Mushroom,' he added. 'Come on, it's getting cold.'

We ate.

Later, in bed, Nicola and I talked. We went round in circles. What, why, where and who were the questioning words we used, but we had no answers.

'We're deserting Daimler,' she said at one stage.

'And other things,' I pointed out. I'd already compiled a list in my mind. 'Barney, don't forget him.'

'Do you think, Emma, when we get wherever it is, we can get Daimler back?'

'I don't know, Nicola. Maybe that would be difficult. It's got a number so they could trace us – '

'Not they,' she corrected me. 'The Gorgon.'

'Yes, the Gorgon could trace us.'

After a while, we drifted into our private silences. From down below in the hotel, there came the sound of dance music, drums and a moaning saxophone. There was comfortable, well-fed laughter and, outside in the car park, doors slammed as people said goodnight to each other.

They were all leading normal lives too, laughing their way home to everyday things: putting the cat out, leaving a note for the milkman. Had Mum cancelled our milk? And the papers? What about our mail? Would it ever reach us?

All these things to be thought of. If the Gorgon was so all-powerful, so determined and with so much money to spend, he could buy almost anyone. Information from this person, a forwarding address from that one.

'Emma?' Nicola said quietly. 'Are you awake?'

How could I not be awake? I pretended to be asleep. Then in the half-darkness of the room, I heard Nicola picking up the phone. It was a push-button phone and she dialled the number slowly, feeling her way as a blind person does. One-two-three, the numbers go across the top. The next row is four-five-six. To help work out your bearings in the dark, there's a little raised pimple on the five button.

I heard the purr-purr as the phone rang at the other end. Then there was a nasal voice, sounding sharp and officious.

'Sorry,' Nicola said, after a pause, then meekly hung up.

'Who were you ringing, Nicola?'

'Francine.'

'At this time?' I said. Francine was her friend from school.

'It's only half past nine. She'll still be up.'

'Was that Francine's mum?'

'No, woman from downstairs. On the switchboard. Silly cow.' Nicola imitated the woman's voice. 'I've been instructed not to connect any numbers from your room.' She snorted again. 'Silly cow.'

'Don't be rude, Nicola,' I said.

We were incommunicado. Locked away from the world. But it was for our own safety. I knew that now. Obviously Nicola would need a little more time before it properly sank in.

In the morning we got up, showered, dressed and ate what they called a continental breakfast, which had been delivered on a tray. Tea, toast and jam, then with our packed bags we went downstairs to the foyer.

Normally, Dad would break off and attend to the bill, but the policewoman had already taken care of it. In the car park was a green mini-bus with tinted windows, which had enough room for all of us, plus our pathetic little bags. Was this all we were to be allowed to have with us? I wondered.

There was a driver and another man, both in plain clothes, both policemen, I gathered. I didn't recognise them from the night before and I hoped that Dad had checked these two out – asked to see some identification.

Already it was affecting me – the way you had to think before you did anything. It was to be the way of the future, or at least until this business came to an end. And what sort of end would that be? The thought made me shudder.

It was half past seven when we drove out of the car park. Twenty to eight when we said farewell to Knutsford, sweet little town full of history – and a small part of ours too, the Cassidy family who used to be from Timperley, but not any more. The driver knew our future address, but we didn't.

'Dad, what's our new name again?' Nicola asked innocently.

'Morton,' Dad supplied the name.

'That's good picking.' She turned away to look out of the window. 'Mort's French for dead. Good choice.' She started to cry and Mum tried to hug her, but Nicola would not be consoled.

At ten to eight we picked up the A50 and headed south. It had started to rain again, streaking obliquely down the windows. In a way the rain was a blessing. It distorted our features so we'd not be recognised by any passing criminal.

I knew then that we'd all have to think of such things, all the time.

As we drove, I thought too of Sandra, who'd have been looking out for me on the bus we caught to school in the morning. She'd have waited for me, of course, and let the first bus go, which is what we always did if one of us didn't show on time. As each minute passed I kept looking at my watch, trying to guess what would be happening in my classroom at that moment.

Sandra would have reported to our home room teacher, Ms Merryman, that I was absent. No one would think anything of it. Girls were always being reported absent. Then there would be what Ms Merryman called 'our regular bit of housekeeping' – notices and news items. I glanced again at my watch. The first bell would sound just about now and there would be the usual clatter and talk as we moved to the English room where Ms Sangster would take us through the morning. Maybe Sandra would report me absent for a few more days. Would she ever go around to my place to see what was wrong? Would someone tell the school about our plight? How would they explain my sudden departure to the girls I'd known for five years or more?

What about Barney? The policeman said he'd look after him, but what shape would it take, that 'looking after' of our Barney? (Our pet for seven years. Knew five tricks and if you happened to mention the word 'walk' he almost went crazy.)

Relatives? Both of Mum's parents were dead but we had an uncle, an aunt too, and a couple of cousins, Roger and David. We didn't see each other very often. They lived on the other side of Manchester, in Bury – wow! Another death-association name! I hoped just then that Nicola wasn't thinking of Roger and David too. Or of where they lived. But she'd got over her tears and sat with her head resting against the glass, keeping her thoughts to herself.

We had family friends too, as well as neighbours. Dad had office associates, Mum had colleagues from her work. We always bought our things in the same shops: butcher, bakery and candlestick makery. How soon would it be, I wondered, before they began to ask about us?

And what about 'him'? I had always made a point of catching the early bus to school, because 'he' was usually there. After all those mornings of early rising I never did find out his name, but it would only have been a matter of time. The difficulty about attending a girls' school is that there are no boys. It's the same in boys' schools of course. If education is for life, how can you say life in a girls-only school is real life? Real life is fifty per cent opposite sex. In our school the percentage was zero – apart from a handful of male teachers, who put themselves off-limits, either because of age or downright unattractiveness.

If he and I had gone to the same co-educational school, we'd have broken the ice long ago, probably have grown up together, reaching puberty at more or less the same time. Suddenly our hormones would have taken over, and we'd both have decided we liked what we saw in each other. We'd have had all those years of lovely, common experience to share, so conversations would be easy.

As it was, we only met on the early bus. We got off at the same stop, where he went his way, and I mine.

Sandra knew I was keen and she kept on at me to talk to him.

'If you don't, I will,' she threatened, but I told her she'd be dead if she did. So the situation just went into lull mode.

We always travelled on the upper deck and one morning, a couple of weeks back, he let me go downstairs first. I hung on to the vertical rail to steady myself and he slid his hand down the rail and touched mine. I looked up and he smiled down at me. I smiled up and left my hand where it was until we had to get off. He didn't look back and just went away with his mates, but he wasn't sniggering or boasting to them that he'd touched my hand. If anything, he was subdued. But pleased too. It made me feel good.

Days later, we spoke. Standing on the lower deck at the bottom of the stairs, I hitched my schoolbag higher on my shoulder.

'All this weight,' I said. 'I'll have a permanent stoop.'

'Yeah,' he agreed. 'I'm thinking of getting a trolley.'

'A supermarket trolley?' My eyes widened.

'Only joking,' he said.

I knew he was joking, but he could have carried it on a bit longer. We could have gone through old ladies' shopping trolleys, flight attendants' luggage trolleys, golf buggies, strollers. We could have talked about the strength of character it would take to be the first student to be seen with such a conveyance for our schoolbooks. We could have talked. And talked.

With the ice now well and truly broken, he'd have been really keen to see me on the early bus.

'Where are we going?' Nicola broke into my thoughts, directing her question to no one in particular.

'South of here,' the driver answered. 'Got a nice little house for you.'

'Where?' Nicola was not put off.

'Bit south of Stoke-on-Trent.'

That started me thinking again. If she'd known we were going there, Ms Sangster would have been pleased, for Stoke-on-Trent is right in the heart of Arnold Bennett country. He was another of her favourite authors, the one who wove into his novels the five towns that made up present-day Stoke-on-Trent. The city has always been famous for producing pottery and fine porcelain, including some well-known names – Minton, Wedgewood, Copeland and Spode. Mum had a couple of pieces of Spode china; very small pieces, but they were genuine Spode.

As the crow flies, Stoke-on-Trent is only some fifty kilometres south of Manchester and about two hundred and sixty north-west of London, but on the heavily congested A50 that morning, we were not flying like a crow or like any other winged creature. Patches of fog slowed us to a crawl, and we were held up by a truck that had overturned, shedding its load across two lanes.

'You'll be safe enough.' The second policeman broke into my thoughts. 'As long as you live, eat and sleep security. Look left, look right and over your shoulder – '

'Someone'll be there to give you the drill,' the driver cut him off. I saw him give his mate a quick, frowning look. He drove on for a minute then said in a softer voice, 'It's hard at first – '

'You've done this before?' Mum asked.

'Relocations? Yeah, many times.'

'Trouble is, you're left on your own,' his mate in the passenger seat started up again. 'We got the witness protection scheme going but right now, we're not very big on follow-up. Know what I mean?'

'Counselling?' Dad asked. 'Support?'

'Yeah. No one tells you what you're in for.'

'When can we get our own things?' Mum asked. 'Furniture, clothing?'

'Tricky, that,' the driver's mate said. 'See, if you were just hiding out from a local hard-man who's stiff-armed someone outside the pub, then that's one thing. A hard-man's just a hard-man, got plenty of muscle, maybe a few mates to put the frighteners on you, but that's about all. Now the sort of individual you've tangled with, he's something else.'

'Like Boots the Chemist,' Dad murmured. 'Branches everywhere?'

'Yes. So if we're to move your furniture, it means we call in outside firms. That makes a weak link. Know what I mean?'

'It might lead him or his cronies to where we live?' Dad asked.

'Tricky,' the man agreed. 'Know what I mean?'

'So let things lie as they are for the moment,' the driver added. 'That's the best advice.'

'Yes.' Dad nodded.

We skirted the city, which in the grey mid-morning air looked pretty gloomy. Our destination was some little way south of Stoke-on-Trent, in a small town called Illing-worth. More of a village really, so don't look for it on the map, unless you use a very big one. We drove along its main street, which had the usual cluster of shops, a pub, and some houses, and soon we were into open country again. All I can say is: it wasn't Timperley.

Nor was our new house anything like the one we'd just vacated. The driver and his mate helped us inside with our bags, wished us all the best, then went back in their mini-bus to wherever it was they came from, leaving us to explore the place. From the outside it looked more-or-less like the house next-door, and the one on the other side too. It stood on its own plot of land, so it had a back and front garden, although grass had not yet been laid. Inside, there was some evidence of the builders not having cleaned up properly after themselves, smears on the windows, that sort of thing.

The house had three bedrooms, a living room, a kitchen and a laundry. The place was furnished simply, and someone had supplied crockery and the usual things we'd need. The larder contained tins of food, and a wrapped loaf of sliced bread stood on the table, but it was white bread, which none of us ate. There were cornflakes in a packet and a bottle of milk in the fridge.

Some kids ran by in the street outside, making a loud noise. Mum winced. None of us spoke as we took in our new home. It fell to Dad to break the silence, almost defending himself.

'They can't give us a palace,' he reasoned. 'Their policy's not to give us better than what we had, otherwise the other side's defence lawyers will say the police have bribed me.'

'There's no television,' Nicola spoke up. 'How will we watch *Neighbours*?'

'We'll hire one,' Mum said. 'Now, let's make the most of what we have.'

'They said someone would meet us,' I pointed out. 'To give us the drill.'

Even as I spoke, we heard a car draw up outside. A sudden terror overtook me. What if this wasn't the one who'd give us the drill? What if it was someone else?

Dad went out to meet whoever it was.

3

They were plain-clothes police, a man and a woman, the man from the local station and the woman from Manchester CID. Dad made sure they were genuine before allowing them in, although they didn't show their identity folders until they were actually across the threshold, with the front door closed behind them.

The woman explained that showing identification the way they do on *The Bill* is a dead give-away. If the neighbours thought they were real estate people or Jehovah's Witnesses, then so much the better.

'Could we talk?' the woman began, looking directly at Nicola and me in a way that said she didn't mean us to be present. She took a folder from her briefcase and dropped it on the dining room table. 'We have a check list of things to sort out, from financial matters to personal security.'

'Yes,' Dad agreed, then to us, 'look, um, girls, what say – '

'Oh, I've got a check list of my own,' I said with just a hint of sarcasm. 'A *thousand* things to do. Unpack, tidy my room – '

'Don't make it hard, Emma,' Mum cautioned me, with a you're-a-big-girl-now tone. She steered us both out of the living room, then dropped her voice. 'We've got quite enough on our plates, haven't we?' She gave my shoulders a firm squeeze, so I suppose she did the same to Nicola on the other side. It was nice to be gently *considered* like that, to know that our mother was aware of what we were both keeping to ourselves – the absolute *mountain* of awfulness.

In the privacy of the hall, Mum held us both. After what seemed to be too short a time, she let us go.

'We can handle it,' Nicola said.

'That's the way. Be tough.' She gave us a wink, which was uncharacteristic. Mum was never a good winker, Dad always said.

So we left the grown-ups to talk through their check list. We'd learn what we needed to know soon enough – although I wanted to be there, finding out everything right now, putting questions of my own. As it was, Nicola and I spent minutes deciding who'd have which of the two smaller bedrooms. Both had single beds with folded linen and blankets on them, a dressing table and mirror, and a built-in wardrobe. I had a feeling that it didn't matter who had which room. Surely this wasn't going to be our future?

The view from my bedroom was of the backyard, which had been roughly turned over by some kind of rotary tiller. There was a wooden fence, and beyond that some straggling bushes, then a flat expanse of grassy meadow, which would soon become building plots. It had started to rain again.

Mum had packed my bag for me, in a hurry obviously, for things that I'd have brought with me had been left behind. My diary, for example. Someone will find that, I thought, and probably read it. Not that I'd written anything I'd be ashamed to own, but it was private all the same. I'd started mentioning the boy on the bus, *that* sort of private.

But Mum had her losses too, as I found out when we talked later. She'd forgotten to bring the photo albums, which showed us in all our stages of growing up. Our whole lives in coloured, postcard-size prints, matt finish, all neatly preserved behind clear plastic film.

Even today, I cry when I remember one particular photo. It was one of us, the Cassidy family, on a wintry afternoon – all of us rugged up, smiling cheesily, Daimler in the background. That day, Dad had brought the car out for a wash and a polish, not that it was needed. He rarely used it.

Daimler had belonged to a client – not the Gorgon, a decent client from our early Timperley days, when Nicola and I were in primary school.

When the client died, Dad was genuinely sorry, but some time later he came home and announced that he'd inherited a car. We were thrilled. We'd never met anyone who'd been left something in a person's will.

'It's not just a car,' Dad explained. 'It's a Daimler.'

'Fancy us in a Daimler,' Mum said. 'We'll need to employ a chauffeur. Or at least buy you the proper hat, Don.' But the Daimler, when it arrived, was an old one from the sixties. 'M-mm.' Mum was doubtful.

'Not old,' Dad protested. 'Venerable. It's a beauty. A classic.' The Daimler was black, with huge silvery headlights and a long bonnet. The bodywork, engine and leather seats were in remarkable condition.

Since it was rarely used, Nicola and I often spent our time in the back of Daimler, with our dolly tea-sets spread out on the carpeted floor. On other occasions we dressed up, wore cooking-foil tiaras and practised our regal waving. The fun we had!

The photo in the album captures another fond memory – what we were doing, what we said, and what we thought even. With the camera on a tripod, Dad posed the three of us against Daimler. Then he spotted something.

'Wait,' he commanded. 'I've got to fix that wheel.' The D insignia on the front hub was at an oblique angle. We waited, teeth chattering, while Dad got out the jack and lifted the wheel to adjust the D.

'Are you going to do that every time you park?' Mum demanded but, despite our protests, Dad wouldn't be crushed. He put the jack away, pressed the self-timer on the camera, and dashed to join us.

'Don't forget to smile,' he said. We did – in fact, we giggled. Every picture tells a story.

It had been an enormous thought to take in, the idea that back in Timperley there was a complete family home with our cars in the garage, leftover food in the fridge, unfinished laundry, unwashed dishes on the draining board: all the signs of a fairly happy family life going on. Now it was a *Marie Celeste* of a house, with its occupants vanished from the face of the earth.

There were no coat-hangers in my wardrobe, but Nicola had packed for herself, so she'd brought enough hangers for her own clothes. Since cajoling didn't work, we had a fight, Nicola saying I should have got home early and packed for myself and no, she didn't like the idea of putting two things on one hanger.

'Look, it's only until we can get things sorted out, Nicola,' I reasoned with her. She relented and I got three hangers, two wooden and one of the wire type that you get from the dry-cleaners – but none of Nicola's fancy ones with knitted covers, because she'd made them herself.

It was all so stupid and impossibly infantile. So much energy and emotion expended on pointless arguments over coat-hangers!

Bloody!

Of course we had fights. What sisters don't? Only the week before we came away, we'd had a humdinger. It was because Nicola had taught Barney a new trick. She had him sit up and beg, which he could do anyway – but her new refinement was to balance a Meaty Bite on the dog's nose and say, 'Stay.' Then she said, 'Attack', and Barney tossed the Meaty Bite up, then caught it and ate it.

It was a great trick – only he wouldn't do it for me, so I flounced off in a huff.

'Come and I'll show you how to do it, Emma,' she relented. What's the point of having something to show off if your audience disappears?

41

'Don't want to,' I said airily. 'Other things to do.'

'You do want to.'

'I don't. I mean, teaching a poor defenceless dog to perform demeaning tricks. Robs him of his dignity.'

'Ho, what a load of old cods' socks. Who was it taught him to roll over?'

'That was different. I was younger then and didn't know any better. About your age.' I added that bit to rile Nicola, but it didn't work.

'Come on, Barney,' she said, and went away to try him with another Meaty Bite.

I never did get Barney to do that trick. I suppose, whatever happens to him, all his tricks will die out and be forgotten, because no one is ever going to put him through his paces. Atrophy is a word I read that means to wither away from lack of nourishment. So all his trick knowledge will atrophy.

The only thing left to do was to make up my bed, then lie on it with hands behind my head, all the time thinking of that word. I would atrophy too, not from lack of food – I'd get that all right – but from lack of the other things that sustained me.

I composed a check list.

We had some lunch, white bread sandwiches and tea, followed by a family meeting or council of war, as Nicola called it. The police had gone, but that wasn't to be the end of their interest in us. Dad was an important witness for them so they would continue to liaise, they promised.

Dad had numbers to ring, including a special emergency number – not the regular 999, but another one.

The house didn't have a telephone, which seemed to me an oversight, but I knew Dad had his mobile phone so I thought we'd be able to use that. Even there I was wrong.

The police had taken the mobile phone, another precaution. Dad could be traced through it, don't ask me how – it was just them being thorough. Apart from that, the first thing Dad told us was that he didn't expect us to forget the life we had in Timperley, but we were to put it on hold. We were never to try making any kind of contact with the friends we had back there, so the phone was a no-go area.

'Look, girls,' Dad said. 'You're both fairly mature now. Your Mum and I have given you a free rein, lots of responsibility, and you've both been tremendous with it.'

I knew that anyway.

'But now it's time for us to tug on the reins,' Mum went on. 'It's going to be hard, being fugitives like this, making do in this place, building up again – '

'What about the Honda?' Nicola put in.

'We'll just have to wait and see,' Mum said. 'Both cars will have to be sold, too risky to keep them otherwise. When we get the funds, we'll see what's what.'

'You mean, sell Daimler too?' I asked.

'Daimler too.' Dad nodded.

Nicola whistled. 'And what about school?'

'Not for a couple of weeks,' Dad said. 'We'll sort ourselves out first.'

'It's hardly worth it,' I pointed out. 'So late in the year.'

'No, better go,' Mum told us. 'It would look odd you two not going to school. See, the thing is, we have to appear as normal as possible – '

'And all the time we're as abnormal as you can get,' I interrupted.

'Have you got a better idea, Emma?' Dad inclined his head, waiting for an answer that I didn't have. Then he smiled. He obviously didn't want to put it in such a challenging way. I smiled back.

There was more, of course. That was only a taste of the awfulness of our changed situation. Taking on a new identity and shucking off the old one isn't as easy as you'd think, with accounts to be settled and closed, credit cards to be paid off and cancelled, magazine subscriptions and club and library memberships to be terminated, and all of this to be done without saying where we were. Nicola and I had saving accounts so they had to be closed, Dad and Mum's accounts too, and the money transferred without telling anyone where we'd gone. Our Timperley house and furniture would have to be sold. Every part of it was so final, making me think that there could never be an end to whatever kind of trouble my father had got himself into – dragging us along with him!

When it came time to start at our new schools, well, we'd have no records to give them, nor list of achievements, neither standing in our previous classes nor references from teachers to say what model scholars we'd both been. We would be unknown quantities, without history or background to speak of. And we'd need an excuse, to explain why we were the way we were.

We couldn't whisper to the headmaster, 'Hey look, we're on the run. On the witness protection scheme, don't you know?' Then he'd nod wisely, tap the side of his nose, give us a wink and promise never to breathe a word to anyone. Except his wife, maybe, and a couple of really close friends at the club. And maybe his wife might just mention it at the hairdresser.

I had a mental image of myself, standing in the centre of all the bits and pieces that had been my Timperley life. I had a large pair of scissors in my hand and I began to revolve on the spot, all the time cutting, snipping, lunging at this memory or that, shearing off great chunks of my past. As I turned it became darker, until I had cut away every single vestige of what had been.

Only drabness remained. Limbo.

The one advantage that I could see was that we had little to unpack. Mum and Dad did theirs, then we explored the other domestic arrangements in the place.

The food situation was awful – only tins of things like soup and vegetables. So, before it got properly dark, we set out together on a shopping trip. On foot.

In the old days, before this happened, we'd go to our

own shopping centre in Timperley, which was as familiar and unchanging as you could wish. If ever a shop closed down it would be the talk of our dining room table, with conjecture about what the new shop would be called, what it would sell. We knew every shopkeeper and assistant. In fact, Nicola and I had nicknames for some of them, including the two girls in the deli.

'Who was it served you?' I'd ask my sister. 'Was it Grumpy?'

'No, it was Scratch.'

Grumpy never spoke except to state the price and maybe say, 'Anything else?' or 'Next'. Scratch seemed to be in a permanent state of itchiness, around the edges of her tight bra in particular, but she always put on plastic gloves before handling the meat. I'll give her that.

I'd miss them all. Grope, Spots and Leer too – and all the cruel fun we had at their expense. Giving nicknames was a Nicola 'thing'.

'One day, someone'll do it to you, Nicola,' Mum said, but that didn't deter her.

There was a shopping centre three streets away from our new house but it was no more than a group of typical small-town shops, a bookshop, a chemist, a betting shop and the target of our expedition, a small self-service store. We invaded *en famille*, as they say, because Mum and Dad wouldn't leave us behind or let us out of their sight. We hurried through our shopping then walked home.

Each of us had a couple of plastic bags to carry. Nicola and I went on ahead with Mum and Dad watching over us.

'*Neighbours* is on,' Nicola said.

'No, it's tomorrow night,' I corrected her. *Neighbours* was almost a religion in Manchester. Everyone loves it because you hurry, through the cold and the growing darkness, to the brightness of *Neighbours*, where it never rains. In Ramsay Street, people just walk in and out of each other's houses. So friendly.

'Makes no odds either way,' Nicola said. 'There's no television.'

'Put it on the list,' Dad said from behind.

'And a CD player?' I asked. Dad only grunted.

Our next-door neighbour was out at his front gate, standing under the streetlamp reading the *Evening Sentinel*, which had just been delivered.

'Evening,' he said as we went past. He was forty or fifty, wore dark, baggy pants and a cardigan, and was going bald. He didn't look like a threat, but neither did Hitler.

'Yes, hello,' Dad returned the man's greeting.

'Just moved in then?'

'This morning,' Dad agreed.

'Need anything? Pots, pans?'

'No, the agent fixed us up with most of the stuff we need.'

'Yer, there's been a lot of to-ing and fro-ing,' the man said. 'A lot of activity. I said to the missus, there's new folks moving in and when you showed up this morning, "What did I tell you," I said.' There was a note of triumph in his voice.

'Yes,' Dad smiled and nodded. Mum fumbled for the front door key.

'Got a couple of young 'uns too.' The man observed us as if we were fat lambs. 'Our George'll be pleased. Pair of kids his age. Nice.'

'We have to get in,' Dad said, and we left the man at his front gate, still pretending to read his evening paper.

'Oh, George and Emma,' Nicola breathed the names once she got inside. She closed the door then stood with her back to it, a silly, rapturous expression on her face. 'Sounds dead romantic.'

'Shut up,' I said. Our parents smiled, and began unpacking the shopping.

Dad hired a television set, and brought home a new mobile phone, which made us all feel safer at night. Without actually taking us with her to check the place out, Mum had made inquiries about our new school. Our parents didn't announce it as some kind of strategy, but I noticed they never ventured out together. That would mean leaving us at home on our own, which often happened in our old place – but not now. At the same time, when either of them did go out, they'd say exactly where they were going and how long they expected to be away.

From this precaution, I could tell it would be a long time before Nicola or I would be allowed out on our own, so there was no point in pressing the matter.

Mum and Dad took us to one of the southern suburbs of Stoke-on-Trent to buy what we'd need for the new school in our local area, a council school. At least there would be boys, and I'd have my other fifty per cent of the population. But now I wasn't so sure I wanted them, nor the fifty per cent that comprised my own sex either. I didn't want this school at all.

On the way back, our neighbour, George's father, was out front again and addressed us in his friendly inquiring way.

'Settling in?'

'Fine, thanks,' Dad answered.

'My missus'll pop over some time. Give you the lie of the land. Shops and that.'

'I'm afraid,' Mum started to say, 'I'll be starting work soon – '

'You're Australian, are you?' The man swung his attention to Dad.

'Um – well – ' Dad hesitated.

'Thought so,' the man winked smugly. 'Can always tell. The way you speak. Aussies, from the telly, see. The ads and that. Down under. Woolloomooloo. Didgeridoo.'

'Yes,' Dad agreed. He nudged me forward, and we left the man smiling after us.

'Fair dinkum?' he called after us. 'That's what your lot say, isn't it? Fair dinkum?'

'Something like that,' Dad confirmed. We went into the house and closed the front door. Our neighbour had found out something about us.

'When did he hear you speak, Don?' Mum demanded. 'You've only ever said half-a-dozen words to him.'

'I don't know.' Dad was angry and upset. A couple of

weeks ago, we'd have laughed. Maybe Nicola would have invented a nickname for the man next-door – Ferret or Nose-job. But he'd shown us how easy it is for people to worm their way in.

His wife too, she'd be coming around, not taking no for an answer – unless we were rude to her. Then they'd say we were stuck up. That way you make enemies, which gets you talked about in the neighbourhood, and during the last war, you know what they used to say about careless talk?

Careless talk costs lives.

There was worse to come and three nights later, come it did. We were in bed. It was late, but despite the hour I was awake, lying in the darkness, going over things in my mind. Nicola and I were not looking forward to the following week, because we'd have to start at our new school. There wasn't a uniform, which suited everyone – after all, this house was only a temporary staging post. In time, and once we had some money, we'd move to a house and a town that we had chosen. Liaising with the Manchester CID, of course.

One of the truly hateful things about being in this place was that we'd had no say in it. Once we were able to assert ourselves we'd feel better, so the fact that there were no uniforms to buy was a bonus. We could cope with any school, knowing it was only for a few weeks at most.

My thoughts were interrupted by George. I had never

actually seen George from next-door, but he had a motorbike, one of those little putt-putt two-stroke things that makes blue smoke and a lot of noise. He'd obviously been out somewhere, the boozer probably, or night school, because I heard him come putt-putting home, then his engine died, and in the still night air I heard him push the bike through their creaking front gate, which banged shut behind him.

Somewhere a dog barked. I drifted off to sleep.

I awoke to hear the dog still barking. My bedside clock radio, which Mum had remembered to pack, told me it was half past two. The dog barked louder, with shorter pauses between barks. Not aimlessly this time, not barking at the moon, but urgent, alarmed and insistent. There was someone there. About two, maybe three, houses along from us.

'Shurrup!' a man's voice snarled clearly. The dog made a terrified yelp and was quiet.

Dad and Mum's bedside light went on, and Nicola raised her voice to ask what was happening. I got out of bed just as Dad came past my bedroom door, tying the cord of his dressing-gown, the mobile phone in his hand.

'Back to bed, Emma,' he said.

'What is it, Dad?'

'Someone having a row. Don't worry.'

A car started up and its engine revved impatiently.

'Come on then if you're coming,' a man's voice almost screamed. A house door shut with a loud thud, then the car door slammed as the car took off, working

51

quickly through the gears until its noise receded. From a distance, I heard it slow down before taking the turn that led to the main road, then it was away. From two doors along, a woman's voice rose in fear. She was outside of her house, in the front street, crying but not forming intelligible words.

Another man's voice carried in the night air, from across the road.

'Here, wha's up? What's all that din, eh?'

'Help!' The woman found words to say. 'Oh, help me here! He's bleeding!'

Dad was already on the mobile phone. I joined him at the front door, wearing my slippers and dressing-gown. He broke away from his call.

'Back inside, Em.'

'What is it?'

'Disturbance,' was all he would say. Then he walked out into the front garden so I'd not hear what he had to report.

There could be no more sleep, not for any of us. Soon the night was filled with flashing blue lights. An ambulance stood with doors open. Heavy set, uniformed figures came and went from the house along the street. Neighbours were out, huddled at their front gates, their breath condensing in the cold air. The man from next-door was there, with a taller figure. This was George.

Mum joined us in the kitchen, then Nicola came too, and we made tea.

'Well,' Mum said. 'Never a dull moment.' She tried to make light of the incident – until there came a knock at the front door. Mum stiffened. She had just taken a spoonful of sugar, and froze with it between bowl and cup. 'Who could that be?'

'I'll get it.' Dad rose.

'No!' Mum spoke sharply.

'It's all right,' Dad assured her. 'Half the Staffordshire constabulary's out there. I'm expecting him.' He went to the door and seconds later came back with the plain-clothes man who'd turned up on the day we arrived.

'Nothing to worry about. Domestic situation.' He might have said more, but for the presence of Nicola and me.

'Tell me this,' Dad sat the man down and put a tea cup in front of him, 'are those people on a witness protection scheme too?'

'You don't expect me to respond to that!' The policeman flinched from the shock of Dad's question. But his body language gave us the answer.

'Tea?' Mum held up the pot.

Then Nicola put another proposal to him. 'Maybe it was us they were after.'

'No sugar,' the policeman said. But he sat with his head down, gnawing on his bottom lip.

'Is that a "no"?' Nicola went on. 'Or are you calling me, "Sugar"?'

'Nicola!' Dad frowned, but the policeman looked up and smiled.

'I don't want any sugar.'

After half an hour, the commotion outside settled down and the policeman left.

'What will Next-door Nosey think of us having a visitor at this time of night?' Nicola asked. 'I bet he took it all in.'

'Just another damned excuse we'll have to invent.' Mum got up from the table. 'Well, we can't live our lives like this.' She paused. 'We really can't.'

Inwardly I cheered, but Dad sat stone-faced. We were ganging up on him, which we'd often done in the past – but those were jokey affairs, the girls against the boy. In fact, we'd had one last Sunday morning, before all this nonsense broke over us, with Mum leading the attack and Dad cowering in mock surrender. But this was a serious ganging up.

'Lil, do you think I don't feel it?' With his hands wide, Dad made his appeal to all of us. 'Maybe it's an old-fashioned notion these days, but I see myself as provider, protector – '

Mum made only the slightest shrug, a dismissive action that Dad noticed straightaway. Then it was his turn to shrug. He just folded both hands into his lap, which made it Mum's cue. She softened her voice.

'Don, I know you can't help any of this – '

'Understatement.'

'But that business along the street – the police won't even tell us the truth about it. Was it a domestic dispute or was it – ' Mum paused. 'Was it us they were after? A wrong house situation?'

54

'And this whole street,' I spoke what was on my mind. 'Are we all protected species?'

Then Dad absolutely floored us.

'What would you girls think,' he said, 'if we went to live in Australia?'

4

Well of course, after Dad's suggestion there was nothing but the wildest ecstasy in that kitchen. Nicola was all for packing right there and then. Dad had to calm her down in case Next-door Nosey heard the commotion she made. Already, Mum's attitude was different; this was a positive step, it was doing something for ourselves. Up to this point we'd been directed this way, shepherded that way, warned what not to do, but with Dad's sudden announcement it was as if we were fighting back, taking control of our own lives again.

There was no more sleep for us that night. We sat in the kitchen talking about the prospect of Australia, until at last Mum and Dad, both of them more cheerful now, shooed us off to bed. But even there, Nicola and I maintained our enthusiasm. I'd have let it go, but Nicola came flopping into my room, wrapped in her blanket, and sprawled across the end of my bed.

'Just think, Emma,' she breathed in the darkness. 'Australia.' We became caught up in our dream of bright, and endless sunshine, smart beach clothes and suntans, vivid Ken Done colours, plus all the sophisticated stuff we'd seen on television. (Because of Dad's background, Nicola and I had long been enthusiastic followers of Australian soaps, documentaries and movies, so we knew it all.)

Nicola's special interest was Australian wildlife, anything that swam, crawled, slithered, flew or hopped. She dithered between what 'ist' she'd like to be when she grew up – entomologist, biologist or zoologist. As she learned more, she began adding specialisms to her future profession.

'I think I'll be a marine biologist,' she'd say. 'Specialising in crustaceans.'

'Oh, yum,' I answered. 'Seafood!'

'Ha!' she sneered. 'Just you wait.' Nicola liked to wait till we were having dinner, then start discussing the more disgusting habits she'd observed amongst the television wildlife, using words like 'regurgitate' and 'pre-digested'. 'Oh, imagine if our mother fed us pre-digested fish,' she'd said one time. 'Must be pretty nourishing, though. Smelly but nourishing – regurgitated shrimps and fish eyeballs. M-mm.'

'Mum!' I pleaded. 'Nicola's being thoroughly obnoxious.' But Mum was never on my side when Nicola let loose. She's also mistress of the straight face, is Mum.

'Eat your squid, Emma,' she said.

'Oh, not you too?' I exploded, pushing my plate away.

After the excitement of the night came the reality of the morning. The immediate drawback was that in our new 'safe' house we had little in the way of information about Australia. Back home, as we still called our house in distant Timperley, we had picture books and magazines, but here we had nothing to satisfy our thirst for enlightenment. Except poor old Dad's memory.

'Where will we live? What will our house be like?' We plied him with questions. 'What city?'

'I'd like Sydney,' Nicola put in her bid. 'Near the sea.'

'Whoa,' Dad laughed. 'One thing at a time. Nothing's settled. I have to clear it with the police in Manchester.'

'Yeah, the witness thing,' I conceded. 'Should be okay though. Easy enough to come back and sort out the Gorgon.'

'I'm glad you've got it all worked out, Emma,' Mum spoke up. 'It's more than just that – there's immigration. Will they let us in?'

'Dad's Australian,' Nicola pointed out the obvious. 'Piece of cake.'

'Well we can't do anything this weekend,' Dad said. 'But on Monday morning, I'll start the ball rolling. Ring around a few people.'

'Aw,' Nicola showed her disappointment. 'I thought we'd just pack up and go tomorrow, or next week some time.'

'Not as easy as that,' Dad told her. 'We might have to wait our turn.'

'You mean there's a queue to get in?' Nicola demanded. Dad nodded, then held his arms wide to show how big it was.

But even so, the very idea of going to the other end of the world grabbed us all, and held our interest throughout the weekend. Even Mum and Dad had changed. They smiled and were more like their old selves – of only three days ago! Dad said, 'Yair, fair dinkum,' a couple of times, once during Sunday lunch, which was full of questions from Nicola and me, and again in the afternoon. As far as we were concerned, the trip down-under was as good as in the bag, or as Dad used to say, we were home and hosed.

On Sunday evening, we were shocked when Mum reminded us that we had school in the morning.

'School?' Nicola made three distinct musical notes of that word. 'It's not worth going, is it? I mean, if we're flying to Australia – '

'Flying Qantas,' I added.

'Dad's only looking into the possibility,' Mum said. 'So until we find out what's what, we'll just have to carry on as if we're here to stay.'

'I hate this place.' Nicola shook her head. 'It was just bearable, knowing we'd be leaving soon. But now I hate it all over again. I mean, the Gorgon's only in custody. *He* might still get off, but it's like *we're* in prison for the rest of our lives.'

'Don't be silly, Nicola darling.' There wasn't much conviction in Mum's voice and she paused before speaking, as if recognising the reality of what Nicola had said. What we were going through was the price Dad had to pay for telling the truth about the Gorgon. In fact, we all had to pay the same price and we had no say in it.

None of us could dissociate from the family. We were all in it together.

Reluctantly, and with a lot of sighing, we got our clothes ready for the first day at our new school, and had to endure another council-of-war, as Mum and Dad talked about the safety precautions we must take.

For other kids, safety instructions were nothing more than a reminder to look left, look right, then, if the road is clear, walk-don't-run, cross at marked crossings, don't talk to strangers, that sort of thing – but ours were different, more serious. We both had to be actors!

Mum would go with us on the bus, and meet us when school came out. We were never to travel without each other, and we had to concoct a story about where we came from. Since we didn't want to say we'd attended school in Timperley, we 'borrowed' a former school, agreeing to say we'd gone to a council school in Bury, where our cousins lived.

We knew enough about their background to make it sound convincing. Dad said we didn't have to volunteer information, only give it if we were asked. The idea was to be friendly but not too forthcoming, not to be stand-offish. For a while, we were never to accept invitations to any kind of event, school outings, visits and so on.

Later, Mum said, when we had organised a family car, we could be dropped off to school and picked up in the afternoon.

'Getting a car?' I asked. 'But is it worth it?'

'We'll see,' Dad said. Starting at a new school is bad enough. But having to carry all the extra baggage of subterfuge and downright lies made it worse.

On Sunday night I slept badly.

As it turned out, for me at least, the first day was uncomplicated. We waited with Mum outside the school gates until just before the bell rang. That way we didn't need to do any mingling with the other students, who streamed and straggled their way into school, some on bikes but most on foot. The wait gave me a good chance to size the place up.

It was a medium-to-large school, bigger than our old place, and made up of different kinds of buildings, spread out over a wide area. It had once been a sandstone village primary school, and while the original building still stood, it was now surrounded by newer constructions.

An electric bell sounded, and students who'd been dawdling suddenly became energised. We went straight in and found the office. The paperwork didn't take long because Nicola and I had already been enrolled. Mum had lined things up for us, so the formalities were simple.

Then came the horrible sensation of leaving Mum. Okay, I'm almost a senior. I regard myself as pretty cool and sophisticated, but outside the school office, when Mum said goodbye and hugged us in turn, I was taken right back to my first day in primary school. That horrible, wrenching feeling. It came again when Nicola left to go to her classroom, leaving me walking alone in the empty corridor. Nicola must have felt it too.·

Then came the business of knocking and opening the door of a crowded classroom. All eyes turned in my direction – more boys than girls, so my fifty per cent theory was redundant for a start!

'Emma Morton?' the teacher consulted a note on her desk.

'Yes.' I waited by the door.

The teacher scanned the desks.

'Well, sit um – ' She pointed. 'There.' I made my way to the desk, going around the far end of the room, rather than down to the front then back up again.

'Wow,' a boy said, and there was a snigger.

'Enough of that,' the teacher frowned.

'Hello,' whispered the girl who sat in the desk next to mine. 'Emma, is it?'

'Yes,' I agreed.

'I'm Christine.'

'Hi, Christine.'

Oh, Australia, I thought at that moment, where are you now that I need you? Your beaches and sunlight, wide open spaces and smiling people from the brochures? I needed *somewhere*. Anywhere but that classroom. Back in my own school, and right at that moment, we had English for the first period, which I liked. A lovely, positive way to ease into the week.

I put my schoolbag on the floor and tried to lift the lid of my desk. It seemed to be stuck, but I knew it should open. When I tugged harder the lid flew up, making a loud noise.

'Sorry,' I said. Someone laughed. The lid had been

stuck down with chewing gum. On both front corners.

I met Nicola at first break. (Back in Timperley we called it 'recess'.) It took ages to find her because I had no reference point – there was just a sea of faces. But then she turned up, and we found a sheltered spot out of the wind.

'Horrible,' Nicola said. 'I hate it. Never been so homesick. And not for that place where we're living.'

'It'll get better, Nicky,' I tried to console her. 'Just keep thinking of Australia. It never rains on *Neighbours*.'

'Know what he did?' Nicola went on. 'He only asked me to stand up and introduce myself – '

'But you know all the stuff we talked about – '

'Forgot the name of the stupid suburb, didn't I?'

'Never mind.'

'Made a fool of myself. A big girl like me.' At that moment, Christine came up to us.

'Hello, Emma.'

'Yes, hello, Christine. This is my sister, Nicola.'

''Lo, Nicola.'

'Hello.'

'You getting something to eat, Emma?'

'I'm not bothered,' I answered. I mean, who had an appetite?

'Me neither,' Christine agreed. 'I'm not bothered.'

Now that I could see Christine away from her desk, I realised she was thin, hunched inside her grey wind-cheater. Her hair was blonde and straggly, and she stood with hands in her pockets, lips bluish, shivering slightly against the mid-morning cold. She had nothing more to say, but seemed content just to stand there. It was Nicola who twigged what she was on about.

'Were you wanting something to eat, Christine?'

'Only if you've got it to spare.' Christine appealed with her eyes.

We hadn't brought a sandwich or anything, but we had money for the canteen. It was nearby, and the queue had thinned out. Christine accepted a large sausage roll from us, and through it we made our first friend in that school.

'You're not from here?' she said, nibbling the edge of the sausage roll.

'No, from up north a bit,' I answered.

'Bury,' Nicola told her. 'Do you know it?'

'That's up north, isn't it?' Christine asked. We both nodded.

Day one passed without further incident. We made no more friends, and in the afternoon Mum met us as arranged, a little way down the street from the school gates.

Dad had been active. On the twenty-minute journey home in the bus, we sat Mum in the middle and plied her with questions. Despite Dad being Australian, we'd still have to apply for resident status, as immigrants. It would really be no problem since we three were the spouse and children of an Australian. That was the good news and we whooped inwardly.

The bad news was that it would take time for our

applications to be processed. And there was more – Dad would need to go to an Australian immigration office, and the nearest one was in Manchester.

'Not Manchester!' Nicola and I raised our voices at the same time. 'Dad can't go there. He daren't!' Mum had to shush us.

'There's an office in London,' she soothed. 'Australia House.'

'That's the one,' we whispered. Anything but our father having to make a foray back into darkest Manchester. Apart from that, London seemed a step in the direction we wanted to take. Heathrow Airport was in London. It was where the big Qantas jets came and went.

Especially went.

When we got home, Dad was still on the mobile phone, which he'd used so much he had to stop and recharge the battery halfway through the day. The Manchester CID were doubtful about the idea of their main witness taking off all the way around the world. It would present problems for them.

'I'll get a fax machine,' we heard Dad say. 'You can telephone, and I can hop back here within forty-eight hours if need be.'

We left him to his negotiations and raided the kitchen – after all, we'd hardly eaten all day. Now, with positive things happening, we found our appetites again.

'How was school?' Mum said.

'Don't ask,' Nicola took another slurp of milk.

'Like that, was it?'

'Worse,' Nicola said.

Dad was off the phone, rubbing his ear.

'You've heard of bedsores?' he said. 'Well I've got phonesores.'

'Skip the sob-story, Dad,' I said. 'Spill the beans.'

'The beans don't add up to five,' he reported. 'But here's the score so far.'

Dad told us that, as his family, we'd have no problem about emigrating to Australia, but it would take time, about six months before we could leave Britain. The Manchester CID couldn't say when Dad would be required in court and didn't want him to go to Australia, but admitted they couldn't really stop him.

There was also the expense to be considered, but Dad's accountant brain got into gear. The police already had the expense of protecting us, relocating us and so on; all they had to do was convert some of that expense to shifting the four of us to Australia, and Dad's flight back again when it came to the court appearance. Dad would look after the living expenses once we were in Australia. The Manchester Police said they'd think it over, but they weren't happy.

After that, we had glum faces, and sat slouched around the kitchen table, chins cupped in our hands, toying with the biscuit crumbs we'd shed, letting our postures go any old way. Sighs were the order of the day.

'But.' Dad held up a finger. 'I'm working on another idea.'

'Well, don't sit there,' Nicola urged him. 'On the phone! Ring up!' Dad pointed to his ear.

'Gone deaf,' he said. 'Besides, I need to work out a few things.'

So that's where we left it.

Days passed, and there was still no progress on the immigration front, which was a good example of bureaucracy in action – or inaction. The forms hadn't even arrived. That first week at school seemed to drag along so slowly. In the old days, I'd often ask where the week had gone. In this school, it was: will this week ever go?

Now that I was enmeshed with the other fifty per cent of the population, I didn't think it was so good after all. At my school, my old school, we girls tended to talk about things. Of course we could be bitchy, aggressive and mean to each other, but we did it with words. At this new school, the boys were all action, and they were loud too. In class, they dominated things, often wasting time with their silly macho showing off.

And don't talk to me about peer group pressure! All right, we girls have it too, making sure everyone conforms, but with the boys it was more open, and there was more hostility. By the end of the first week, I had earmarked a couple of boys who were obviously pretty smart. Raleigh was one of five or six Indian boys in the class, but he was quieter than most of the others. When the teachers asked a question, he never volunteered an answer, but if they asked him directly, which they eventually did, Raleigh would usually get it right.

The funny thing was that Raleigh's response would be followed by some kind of scoffing reaction from the other boys. They'd exchange remarks, make a small hissing laugh or sometimes even explode in disbelief. He'd receive praise from the teachers, but contempt from the boys in the class. Some girls did it too. That seemed to be their way of gaining notice from the boys. This was something new to me.

It sounds horrible to say this, but Christine turned out to be the best kind of friend we could have found. The truth is, before we came on the scene she was a loner, without a single friend in that school, shunned by the other girls in our class. As for boys, well, she had no hope at all. So it dawned on me that as long as we were her companions, no one would want to know us.

It seemed that the boys kept their distance from us too – because of Christine, and the fact that we didn't mix with the other students. We overheard a couple of the other girls talking unkindly to Christine one morning, but she just accepted their remarks, shrugged, and came over to me. To her, this was nothing new. Water off a duck's back.

After we got to know her a bit more, she opened up to us. It turned out that Christine rarely had any breakfast before coming to school so, in a way, Nicola and I literally bought her friendship from the canteen. This was one of the awful parts of the situation we were in – having to think and act like that.

Nicola and I didn't deliberately start out looking for a Christine – it just developed, so we made use of her. Apart from that, she wasn't the friend I'd have chosen. Christine had no conversation, not even about television, which everyone else talked about endlessly. She wasn't very bright and never asked questions about where we came from. She had no curiosity about us at all. Our relationship existed strictly from day one of our meeting. To use a literary term, in our story there was no exposition that interested her, only the here and now.

I often thought that when we went to Australia, it would be a sudden and secret leaving, as it was from Timperley. There could be no saying goodbye, and our going would make poor Christine friendless again, and hungry. In all of the excitement of planning our flight, this was the only thought that gave me concern.

At home on Thursday night, Nicola produced another of her nicknames. She referred to Christine as 'The Fence'. We were in Nicola's bedroom, just the two of us.

'Nicola, what did you call her?'

'The Fence.'

'Why?'

'Well, it's a good name, isn't it? She keeps the others away.'

'That's horrible,' I said.

'I know.' Nicola's face was sad. 'The things we do, eh?'

Dad's other idea was to ask the Manchester CID to use their influence with the Australian immigration people, to convince them that because of the threat to our safety, we were a special case – not exactly refugees but a special case all the same. He had an idea this sort of thing had happened before, at government-to-government level. The CID were mulling the idea over, Dad reported.

'Tell them to mull faster,' Nicola said.

Dad had completely put off the idea of finding any other kind of work, so that he could concentrate fully on our move to Australia. It was all right for him, Nicola huffed, why couldn't *we* just stop at home too? But Dad staying home was one thing; in a place where lots of fathers were out of work that was quite normal. We kids had to keep up appearances by going to school.

In fact, three major events were to take place before we left Illingworth. The first was George from next-door making his move. Not a major event for anyone else, perhaps, but it was the first time a boy had asked me out, so it was pretty major to me.

By the second week at our new school, Mum stopped going with us each way. We assured her we'd come straight home and not dawdle and that if there should be some kind of delay, we'd ring right away.

It was a big concession, suddenly to be allowed out without Mum riding shotgun, as Nicola described it. In the good old Timperley days, we'd long been able to go to the city on our own, Saturday mornings being our favourite. We'd catch one of Manchester's sleek new Continental-style trams all the way to Piccadilly Bus

Station, walk across Piccadilly Gardens to check out John Lewis or Debenhams, pop into the big HMV music store to see what was what in the latest CDs, then go on up the escalator into Arndale Shopping Centre for some serious looking and trying-on of gear. Great!

So on the afternoon when George made his move, Nicola and I were on the bus home from school. It always passed the local shopping centre, then turned right, and we'd get off at the stop near the head of our street. Then it was only about a three hundred metre walk to our house. But on Tuesday afternoon, Nicola blew it.

At the shopping centre, she jumped up suddenly.

'I've got to get off here, Emma.'

'No.' I was alarmed. 'You mustn't.'

'I want to buy a book – '

'A book? Why?' But Nicola had already started going downstairs with the other passengers. There was nothing for it but to grab my bag and join her. In seconds, we were on the pavement, and our bus had groaned away. Already it was growing dark. Cars had their lights on and shop windows were bright with Christmas decorations. 'Why a book, Nicky? And why can't it wait till Saturday?'

'I need it now. It's for Christine.'

'Christine?'

'Her birthday's tomorrow.'

'Oh, Nicky, why didn't you say?' I relented. All of a sudden my sister had come out with a nice thought, a touching gesture towards Christine that made me feel like Ebenezer Scrooge in his bah, humbug days.

'She's never owned a book,' Nicola went on. 'She told me.' I sighed and dug my hands into the pockets of my windcheater.

'You got enough money?'

'Four pounds,' she said. 'Look, Emma, we'll get back there, what, maybe five minutes late?' Just across the road from the bus-stop was the bookshop, so we walked over and Nicola went in, leaving me stamping my feet to ward off the wintry cold, and realising that Nicola never referred to our new place as 'home'. I didn't either, come to that, and neither did Mum. It wasn't any kind of decision we'd come to – we all did it unconsciously.

'Hello.' Suddenly George was standing in front of me in his dark motorbike leathers and boots. He was half-a-head taller than me, with freckles and tightly curled ginger hair. 'Thought it was you. From next-door.'

'Oh, yes.' I shivered, and looked away from him, as if expecting someone to collect me. I craned my neck to look further into the groups of people.

'Never see you, Emma,' George went on. 'Keep to yourself.'

'Busy,' I answered.

'Still, you gotta get out some time.' He unclipped two press-studs at the neck of his leather jacket. It was his using my name that stung, but I didn't give him the pleasure of knowing that it bothered me. Next-door they must take in every single detail. 'You gotta live a bit, Emma.'

'I live enough,' I said. Keeping people at arm's length

is difficult! I didn't want to sound like some kind of hard-to-get snob. George wasn't bad-looking, although he put on this tough macho act, the way he stood staring down at me.

'There's a dance Friday. Down the youth club – ' I shook my head and smiled, but he wasn't put off. 'Pictures then?'

'Look, um – ' I had no idea what to say. 'Mummy doesn't – '

He gave a short sneering laugh, and picked up that word. 'Mummy?'

I cursed myself inwardly. In this place, 'my mother' or 'Mum' or even 'Mam' would have been all right, but not 'Mummy'. It was as if I'd flashed a badge of rank or something, setting myself apart from George. Luckily Nicola came out just then, carrying a plastic bag.

'Nice wrapping paper too,' she said. 'But can you give me a pound, Emma?'

'I was gonna give you a run home,' George cut in. 'But seeing there's the two of you.'

'Oh,' Nicola said, and looked at George as if he was some kind of gatecrasher. Then she ignored him and went on. 'You know how much a sheet of wrapping paper costs?'

'Come on, we've got to get back,' I said. 'Mum'll create.' As we walked away, George stared after us.

Nicola borrowed the Latin expression that the queen used when she summed up the rotten time she'd had in 1994. 'Anus horribilus,' she observed, keeping her voice low.

'That's annus,' I corrected her pronunciation. 'Ah-noos.'

'I know what I said.'

It was quite dark when we reached the house, but Mum didn't create. She just commented on how late we were. Nicola kept the plastic bag out of sight, so we got away with it.

There was no news from Dad on the exodus Australis front.

Next day, Christine couldn't believe that anyone would, for no reason, suddenly give her something for nothing. Nicola explained it was for her birthday, but Christine couldn't quite grasp the idea.

'For me?' She handled the gift-wrapped parcel as if there was some kind of catch to it. 'It's done up lovely, isn't it?'

'Open it,' Nicola urged her, but still Christine fondled the small parcel, savouring it, turning it over. 'It's only a book,' Nicola went on. 'Paperback, so open it.' She reached out to take the parcel from Christine, but I held her arm.

'Let Christine open it in her own time,' I said.

'It's lovely,' Christine held the parcel in both hands. 'Thanks a lot, Nicola and Emma.' (I ended up paying three-fifths of the cost of the gift, so we had agreed to make it a joint present.) But Nicola's thoughtfulness didn't go unnoticed. Later, when we went into the class-room, one of the other girls saw the gift, which Christine still hadn't unwrapped.

'Who'd go giving you a present?' the girl sneered. Christine only smiled.

'My friends,' she said simply, and put our gift into her desk.

That wasn't the second event that took place. It was just something nice that I wanted to put down. The second event happened on the way home in the bus. There was a man sitting two seats ahead of us, reading the *Manchester Evening News,* which gave me a tiny pang of homesickness. The man moved his arms to turn over to a new page, and I could see the headline on the top left.

Alleged Drug Lord Freed on Bail.

I was sure it had something to do with our situation. It had to be the Gorgon. So that was the second event.

But there was to be a third.

5

Dad took my news about the newspaper headline gravely and talked for ages on his mobile phone, before coming back to the kitchen table where we all sat waiting for him. The look on his face said it all.

'It's him?' Mum asked. 'The Gorgon?' Dad nodded.

'But being in custody wouldn't stop a man like that doing exactly what he wanted. He wouldn't get his hands dirty.'

Still, it was depressing to think that with everything the police had against the Gorgon, they couldn't hold him. But that's the way it works with justice – sometimes it seems the victims are the ones who come off worst in the first place, and when it's all over they're still worse off, sometimes with their lives changed for ever.

Look at us, for example!

'Did the police say anything about supporting our application for Australia?' Mum said.

'Still working on it,' Dad answered.

The only nice thing that day was that the immigration paperwork had arrived in the morning's mail.

Actually, it was the first mail delivery we'd had since

moving into this place. Our new name, Morton, looked strange on the envelope, making me think it was addressed to someone else.

We all passed the application forms around, reading them right through, savouring their words, and the accompanying information leaflets. It went some way, but not a lot, towards taking our minds off the depressing news of the Gorgon's release.

'There was one other thing,' Dad said. We brightened, eager for any little crumb of comfort.

The police had offered to escort Dad back to our Timperley home, to allow him to pack up some cases of personal effects. The rest would be stored for a while, then the police would arrange for them to be delivered later.

'Well, that'll cheer us up,' Mum said.

'They're only doing it to take our minds off going to Australia,' Nicola said.

'Nicola, you're turning into such a cynic,' Mum smiled.

'And she's so young.' Dad shook his head in mock wonder. It was nice to see Mum and Dad being more positive and unified, making jokes and bantering with us, the way they used to in the old days. It's easier to face things if your parents hold together.

I know Mum didn't mean it, none of us had meant it, but we always seemed to be *blaming* Dad for the mess we were in. When something went wrong, we could be quick with our anger, and you'd see the hurt look on Dad's face.

'I've only got a day,' Dad went on. 'So it would just be clothes, books, crockery and personal things. We'll have to sell the heavy items – it would be too risky to transport them.'

'What about Daimler?' Mum asked. 'Any chance, Don?' I was surprised that Mum should be the one to ask about Daimler, but then why not? Of all the things we could have, Daimler was the one permanent symbol of our Timperley life – not because of its swank or its opulence or its Englishness, but for its association with the good times we'd spent together, because we only took Daimler out on special occasions. In fact, every time we planned a trip, the four of us would be involved in the preparation, maybe dusting or polishing the paintwork, or vacuuming the carpets, all the time making sure Barney didn't jump on the seats or shed hairs.

There would always be a delicious sense of anticipation. On Tuesday, Dad or Mum might suggest we go off somewhere the following Saturday or Sunday – maybe to Tatton Park with its mansion and gardens, where we could hire a sailboat or ponies. We'd spend all the rest of the week looking forward to our outing.

Last time we came home from a run in Daimler, I put my monumental proposal to Dad. We had just turned into Stretton Road, which is a long curving street on a slight downhill slope. The car simply coasted along, with hardly a purr from the engine. In this serene tranquillity, I reminded Dad that I'd soon be able to take driving lessons.

'Um,' Dad grunted, then turned on the radio, filling the car with pop music.

'You could learn on Daimler.' Nicola raised her voice, which only caused Dad to growl and turn the radio up even more. He is always very possessive with mechanical things.

'Come to that, Don,' Mum spoke up too, 'when am I going to drive Daimler?'

'Do you think we should have a takeaway tonight?' Dad sank deeply into his seat and made a great show of concentrating on his driving.

'So that's settled then.' Mum nodded decisively. 'Next time out, *I'll* take the wheel.' But there wasn't a next time.

'We don't want Daimler here,' Nicola spoke up sharply, which made us all turn to look at her. She shrugged. 'Not in this place. It wouldn't be right, leaving her parked on the street – ' Nicola couldn't find any more to say, but somehow she was right. Daimler didn't belong here.

'I think it would be too risky to have either of the cars,' Dad spoke gently. 'But maybe one day we'll get another Daimler.'

'But it won't be Daimler,' Nicola said.

'When will you go, Don?' Mum changed the subject.

'This week some time. They'll let me know when they can arrange someone to go with me. So maybe we could all make a list of the must-bring items.'

'My CDs,' I said. 'And diary.' A list would be no problem for me.

'Your school reports,' Mum added. 'We'll need them for Australia.'

'Barney,' Nicola said, but Dad just smiled. Barney was gone, we all had to face that.

'The photo albums.' Mum came up with another idea. 'And all the framed photos from the mantelpiece.'

The third event came with an early-morning phone call. I was in that half-drowsy, half-awake state, and had checked the time so that I knew I could snuggle in for another half hour, when I heard the phone ring.

Dad must have been awake too, for it only rang once. Then came his deep rumble of a voice as he identified himself and said, 'What?' After a pause, I heard him say, 'When did this happen?'

It was bad news – always easy to tell. You don't know the words the other party's saying, but you hear their effect. I got out of bed, wrapped up, then padded along to Mum and Dad's room. Dad already had his feet on the floor, with the bedside light on. Mum was awake too, propped on one elbow. My father's face was like ash as he listened. He caught my eye and shook his head.

Nicola came and stood beside me. Dad sighed, finished his call, and switched off. He breathed out slowly. Mum reached up and put her hand on his shoulder.

'There's bad news and there's worse,' Dad said. His voice was cracking. 'In one sentence – last night, our house was broken into then set alight.'

Beside me, I could feel Nicola slump. There are cliches

such as 'my hopes were dashed', 'my heart sank to my boots' and 'my jaw dropped'. Just then, they all came true.

Nicola cried a little and ran to Mum. I went to Dad and hugged him.

'What did they take?' I asked.

'There wasn't any money in the house, and I brought all of my jewellery,' Mum said.

'Maybe the two things are not even connected,' Nicola offered a word of hope. 'You know, empty house, it would be a sitting target – then maybe the fire started later.'

'They used an accelerant,' Dad told us. 'That's what the fire brigade said.'

'What's that?' Nicola asked.

'Some kind of fuel. A solvent or petrol,' Dad explained. 'And a timing device.'

Whoever it was, they went there deliberately, to start the fire. It wasn't a casual break-and-enter where the fire gets started accidentally, or where they do it because they're angry at not finding anything worth stealing.

'They should arrest the Gorgon all over again,' Nicola said, but Dad didn't answer. He was lost in his own thoughts about what this would mean. We all stayed in that bedroom until Mum and Dad's alarm clock went off, which shook us out of our various states of depression. Then, further along the hall, my alarm sounded, so I went to cut it off.

After that rude awakening, we were like zombies – stumbling around the kitchen, opening cupboard doors, taking mugs from the shelf and filling the kettle.

The horrible thing was not knowing any details – what had been saved and what we had lost. Nor could we go there and get sympathy from our neighbours. We had no car we could jump into and race to the scene, and we had to seek permission before we travelled. If we wanted to move around England, our England, we needed a police escort!

'They'll collect me this morning,' Dad announced. 'I'll have to go and see how bad things are.'

'We're insured, aren't we?' I asked. Dad nodded.

'But that'll take time,' Mum said, with a note of bitterness in her voice. 'You know, the usual delay. The risk factor. Nothing in our life is going to be straightforward again, all this hole-in-the-wall, looking over your shoulder – '

Dad went to Mum with his hands out, but she shrugged him off.

'Look, I'm sorry,' he whispered, but Mum had no words, nothing that would make him feel less guilty about what had happened to our lovely house on Stretton Road, Timperley. Once more, poor Dad was at fault.

I could have gone to him, the way he'd done to Mum, and maybe somehow made it easier for him – but my emotions weren't in check either.

We all sat or stood around in the kitchen until it was time to leave for school. Maybe I learned something that day, I don't know. Certainly, teachers went through the motions of presenting lessons to me, while I wrote things in my book, drew lines and diagrams, read things and even answered the odd question. But if you asked me to tell you a single educational fact that I absorbed that day, then there's nothing I could say.

Back in the house that afternoon, we found Mum still depressed about what had happened. Somehow it made things worse that we couldn't even visit the site to see for ourselves, as if we were expected to mourn a death with no body to grieve over.

'The police have no leads,' was all the information Mum could give us. 'There's evidence of a break-in and the remains of the timer or whatever. Your father's with them now.'

'Your father' – that was ominous. Normally Mum would say 'Dad'. 'Your father' was kept for those times when Mum did what Nicola and I called turning on the Cold Power routine.

In Timperley, even their rows could be jokey affairs.

'Oh, Dad's in the dog house,' we would say. 'Move over Barney. You've got company.'

'Time to grovel, Dad,' Nicola used to advise him. 'With women, grovelling gets you everywhere.'

Then they'd make up. Perhaps Dad would come up behind Mum when she was at the sink or something. He'd growl into her neck, and she'd laugh and shrug him away, maybe splash him with water. His growl would deepen and he'd kick the kitchen door shut, and Nicola and I would exchange meaningful glances.

I used to think, privately of course, that it would be wonderful to enjoy that kind of playfulness with a male – of my choosing, or we'd choose each other, which is important. But this time, the way Mum said 'your father' was bleaker than I ever remembered it.

Ordinary life usually has something in it that you can look forward to, a birthday or other big event. At that time, early December, I'd normally start looking forward to Christmas holidays – the fun of buying presents, maybe a panto in Manchester, then the big day itself and all the festive stuff, followed by New Year's Day. But with what had happened to us, we had seemed to be on a one-way street with no means of turning back. As we went down this wretched thoroughfare, the route was becoming gloomier, seedier, more dangerous even, and as we progressed there appeared to be nothing brighter at the far end.

Except Australia.

I dug out the material that had come from Australia House and read it over, filling in the answers in my mind.

Then Dad came back.

Despite her anger, Mum wanted to know the worst. And it was the worst.

They, whoever they were, had splashed this accelerant substance in all the rooms, so the fire got a good hold and was out of control before any of the neighbours could do anything. Their garden hoses were as pathetic as one of those naughty little plaster gnomes that widdle into goldfish ponds. As it happened, the people on either side of us, the Brierleys and the Maheshwaris, had their work cut out keeping the flames from spreading to their houses. It would have been too horrible if our predicament had affected our neighbours! We'd known them for years, and it was one of Mum's special sadnesses that she'd not been able to say goodbye.

When Dad turned up with the police, Mrs Maheshwari had come around offering sympathy followed by Mrs Brierley, who asked about our sudden departure. They'd heard nothing at all, except for when the house went up and the fire brigade came.

There was nothing that Dad could bring away from the ashes, except the two brass numbers which had fallen off our front door. They were scorched and blackened, with traces of paint sticking to them. Gravely, Nicola took charge of them and went to the kitchen sink, where she grabbed the pot-scourer and the Vim and began scrubbing.

She had her back to us, and the water was running into the sink as she cleaned the muck off. I couldn't tell if it was the intensity of her scrubbing that made her shoulders shake, but when I offered to help she gave the slightest toss of her head, and kept on with what she had to do.

None of us asked about Daimler, and Dad didn't volunteer. But he did go on to say that the Manchester CID had promised to support our application for entry to Australia. It was the only touch of brightness in a very low week.

Something had to come right for us, and by the end of that week, come it did – in the form of another letter from Australia House. The letter stated that in view of our special circumstances, our application was receiving the speediest attention.

Another thing came right, because of an impulse. It was on a Friday. As we were leaving school, we said farewell to Christine. She had read our book three times, she had told us. In fact, every time we saw her, she would tell us a bit more about the story and about how much she enjoyed reading it. She claimed it would always be her favourite book. I believed her.

'And guess what?' she went on. 'I joined the library.' Her eyes were shining.

'That's great, Christine,' I said.

'Lovely and warm in there. Me and my little brother go. He gets books out too.'

At the school gates, Nicola and I always went one way while Christine went the other. Something told me that I needed to make a bigger gesture towards her, to say goodbye in some way, because the day would come soon and there would be nothing worse than just leaving.

'Well, ta-ra then,' Christine said as she made to go off. 'See you Monday.'

'Yeah, goodbye, Christine,' I said, then hesitated. She paused too, trying to work out the expression on my face. Nicola also stood undecided. On an impulse, I hugged Christine and kissed her cheek. Nicola did the same. Christine was very surprised.

'You going away then?' she said.

'It's a long time to Monday.' I laughed. 'I can give my friend a kiss if I want to.'

'That's all right then.' But she was mystified.

'Bye then.' Nicola waved and we went off. At the corner, I turned back to see Christine standing just where we'd left her. She lifted a hand, but didn't wave.

On Saturday morning, there was a plop noise at the front door. I went to the door, and found a brown envelope lying on the mat. Sometimes with mail, the envelopes land address side up. Sometimes not.

This time, there was no address that I could see, although I was looking at the front of the envelope. Long seconds passed before I picked it up, ominous thoughts going through my mind. There was no address on the reverse side either. I opened the front door and looked along the street in both directions, but there was only a woman dragging a small boy by the hand, heads down against the cold December wind. The small boy wanted to skip playfully, but his mother was keen to get on.

'Dad.' I took the brown envelope to him as he sat at the kitchen table. 'This came.' Mum and Nicola were there too.

Dad frowned and felt the contents, wiped the marmalade off his knife, and slit open the top of the envelope. He pulled out a photograph and placed it by his plate.

It was a colour photo of Nicola and me, taken last summer when we went to the beach at Lytham St Annes.

We all stared at our smiling selves, our happy selves, dressed in shorts, T-shirts and sunhats, with Nicola screwing up one eye as if she were winking. It was post-card size, matt finish, and on the back were traces of little parallel brown streaks, still sticky to the touch. The photo lay on the table by Dad's plate. We knew where it had come from.

'That was in our album,' Mum whispered. Her face seemed to have drained of all colour.

Outside the front door, George started up his motor bike and revved the engine. He seemed to be in no hurry to get on, but eventually he kicked the thing into gear and took off. As the sound of his engine died away, Dad looked up at us.

'Right. Pack. We're going.'

'Australia?' I said. Dad nodded.

'We'll sort out the details later. But we're going.'

I packed, Nicola stuffed her bag any old way, Mum gathered the things that she and Dad had brought – and we all did it quickly. I left my bed unmade, my towel on the bathroom floor. On those occasions I'd stayed over at a friend's house, which used to be all the rage when I was thirteen or so, I'd always been careful to strip the bed, tidy the room and to give my host and hostess as little trouble as possible. Mum's influence. But in this place, the sooner I left the better.

Dad spent another hour on the mobile phone, shut away in the bedroom. I could guess that the first call would be to the local police liaison number we'd been given, the next to Manchester CID.

I must have been right, because within half an hour two police constables came to the house. A man and a woman, both in plain-clothes, produced comforting-looking two-way radios then sat in the kitchen, drinking tea and reading the morning paper. They had no idea what it was all about. They were just there to look after us. We waited, dressed for our journey, until Dad emerged from the bedroom to gather us for another conference.

'Um, look,' he said to the constables. 'We've got things to talk about.'

'Don't mind us,' the policewoman said. 'Take your time.' Her colleague was still absorbed in the morning paper and barely looked up. We went into the bedroom. Dad closed the door.

'Right, we're booked on a flight. Leaves tonight.'

'Whew!' It was Nicola who heaved that sigh of relief. '*Neighbours*, here we come.'

'So between now and take-off time, don't leave the house, don't speak to anyone,' Dad said. 'It's pretty obvious they are on to us, so the least said – okay?'

We nodded. I loved that expression, 'take-off time'. If staying silent would move us any faster then I person-ally vowed to clam up until we hit Australia.

We had to wait until our transport came. Once again, it was an ordinary-looking dark-blue mini-bus. It arrived late in the afternoon, as it was growing dark. The driver and his colleague both produced identification, which

Dad checked thoroughly. Then we went out to the bus, carrying our bags.

The man from next door made it his business to be out the front, collecting his *Evening Sentinel* again.

'You folks off then?' he said.

'Yes,' Dad told him.

'That was short and sweet. Missus never even got to say hello.' But no one had time for him, which didn't put him off. He stood watching until we turned the corner at the end of the street.

He might have been the one who put the envelope into our mail slot – or even George. Who's to say? There had been no one in the street, apart from the woman with the skipping child. She could have sent the child to do it – or have done it herself, using the child as cover.

'Wait there,' she might have said. She then runs up to our front door, drops the envelope through the mail slot, then back to the child and off they go together.

Just because she's a woman doesn't mean she's above that sort of thing. When Mum and Dad bought the Timperley house, I was seven or eight. On the day we went to look the place over, the woman who was selling ushered us into the hall, where she left us while she took a cake out of the oven.

We could see her in the kitchen, carefully handling the hot cake tray, slipping it on to a wire rack to cool then she came back to us, wiping her hands on a tea-towel. She showed us over the house, which we all loved. Much later, when the deal was done and we'd moved in and settled, Mum tried the oven and found it didn't work.

'That's strange,' she said, then put on one of her 'penny drop' expressions. Dad just stood there nodding too.

'But the woman baked a cake in that oven,' I pointed out. 'She was nice.' Dad took me by the hand and led me away from the kitchen.

'Emma,' he explained. 'She was a nice-looking woman but it doesn't mean she's above playing little tricks. Nice can often turn out to be nasty. She must have bought that cake ready baked.'

The oven hadn't worked for months, the electrician confirmed. It cost seventy pounds to put it right.

Once we were on the road to London, I lost myself in thoughts such as that one. It was all so easy for the Gorgon – the other side. He had a different logic, plus the people to do his bidding, anonymous manpower, or even womanpower, people beyond suspicion. He had extensive, secret information networks that let him put the word out and receive answers, faster than the police.

It made sense now. The fire at our Timperley house had two purposes – to get information and to draw Dad out of hiding. The Gorgon would have had someone waiting and watching, and this time, the police would not have given them the slip.

Even now, someone could be following us along the busy road, flowing with the traffic, knowing which direction we were taking, always a jump ahead.

The Gorgon was used to thinking like that – with

cunning. His kind of person plots and schemes, whereas our kind of people make naive plans and hope for the best. And when things go wrong for the Gorgon, when he's faced with what he's done, then he can buy the best lawyers to run rings around the prosecution. And the lawyers are nice, honourable, middle-class people, who'll drive their BMWs home in the evening to comfortable houses in fashionable suburbs, where they'll kiss their wives and then listen as little Jeremy or Caitlin report what they did in school that day.

And if their client happens to remove any witness who will speak against them, then it all helps.

It was now dark. We were on the M6, heading south towards the M1 and London, when our mini-bus veered suddenly into a motorway service centre – but we didn't stop at the pumps. We drove around the back and entered a large shed, where no less than four cars were waiting. Two were Granadas, but I didn't properly see the others.

'This is it, folks,' the driver said. His colleague was already out, pulling the side door open, letting cold air spill in. At first I was worried, but Dad squeezed my arm. The place suddenly milled with uniformed police.

'It's okay,' Dad whispered. 'I've been briefed that this will happen.'

They split us up, this time me with Dad, Nicola with Mum. We got into two of the cars, then all four took off, one after the other. The cars branched off in different directions and before long, I had no idea which contained Mum and Nicola. Shortly after that, they were out of sight anyway.

'That'll confuse the buggers,' the driver of our car said. But now we seemed to be heading north again.

'What about London, Dad?' I asked. 'And Heathrow?'

'We're not heading for Heathrow,' Dad told me. 'We'll double back. We're leaving from Stanstead Airport.'

'But we're going Qantas?' I persisted.

'No,' Dad said grimly. 'Not Qantas.'

I settled back in the seat. There was no other conversation, which gave me more time to think.

Christine could have told them about us. Maybe she wouldn't have meant to do it, maybe it was an innocent action on her part, but she could have done it.

See how it affects you? Friends may be enemies.

6

It was late at night when we finally pulled up in front of the departure ramp at Stanstead Airport. For us, there was a special place to stop, so we could get out of the car without being seen. We were not to mingle with other travellers, so they took us to a small, quiet waiting room, which we had to ourselves. Mum and Nicola were already there, with two uniformed policemen and one policewoman. Dad and Mum went off to see the immigration people and attend to travel formalities, leaving us with the policewoman.

'Wish it were me flying off somewhere,' she said with good-natured yearning. 'Somewhere warm and sunny.'

'Yes.' I smiled agreement with her. An automatic smile, the kind you're able to switch on and off.

'Christmas in a lovely tropical place,' the policewoman went on. 'Near the equator, nice.'

All the secretive, furtive skulking and hiding of the last few hours had made me apprehensive and distrusting, and it was pleasant, for a change, just to sit down and relax, knowing that we were safe and would be secure where we were going. As we waited for Mum and Dad to come back, I began to feel the old edge of excitement creeping in.

It wasn't because we were taking a flight. We'd all done that before – Malaga twice, once to Vienna and once to Paris – so we were reasonably used to it. The excitement came from going to Australia.

Dad had often promised us a trip home, as he called it, just as soon as he could wangle enough time away from work commitments, and save the money for the fares. One of my friends at school – my real school – had gone to Australia on a business trip with her parents. She told us when she came back they'd flown business class on Qantas.

'Heaps of room, oceans of drink, mountains of food, in-flight movies,' my friend reported. She watched the movies on her own little personal screen, right in front of her eyes. Later in the flight, she had canted her seat way back, then slept like a log. She produced for our inspection a little kit the attendants issued to passengers – woolly socks, a mask for your eyes, soap, deodorant and toothpaste – which we passed around and admired. 'The whole flight only took twenty-six hours,' my friend concluded. This was the picture I'd built up of how it would be when it was my time to fly to Australia. But that's not quite how it turned out.

Mum and Dad returned, and Nicola and I said goodbye to the policewoman.

'Hope you get your nice tropical Christmas,' Nicola said.

'No, I'll have to make do with London for the next few years,' she answered. 'Goodbye, have a nice flight.'

We still had to get aboard the plane, and although it was only a short distance, there was a sense of unease as we walked through the concourse to the departure lounge. A couple of plain-clothes policemen went with us. There were crowds of people standing around, consulting indicator boards and just looking at the passing scene. Maybe some of them were watching us – just waiting for us to appear. I'd seen a movie where a hit man tried to assassinate someone in an airport, so as I walked there was a horrible, tingly feeling at the back of my neck. We were all silent and subdued, maybe thinking how dangerous this short journey could be.

As we waited to board, I thought about the chain of events that had brought us this far. The Gorgon burns our house, which flushes my father out; the Gorgon discovers where we're hiding, but he's not going to leave it there. Having got this far, he's not going to be put off by a bit of police subterfuge.

We could see our aircraft out on the tarmac. It was to be a charter flight, not with any airline that I recognised. There was some kind of logo on the tail, but the name on the body had been painted out. The plane wasn't a jumbo jet either, but much smaller, one of the Boeings. It was also late taking off, very late in fact. When we boarded, all of the other passengers were already in their seats, leaving space for three of us on one side of the plane, and a seat for Dad just across the aisle. No, it wasn't business class – but it was an aircraft and it was going our way. We settled in as they closed the doors, and there came that expectant hush, before the jet engines began slowly whining up to speed.

At last, we were airborne, lifting into the darkness. For a short time I could see a sprinkle of lights below – houses, shops, streets and traffic, people going about their affairs. Then we passed through the cloudbank and they were all gone. Mum, who was in the aisle seat, reached across and rested her hand on top of Dad's. He just opened and shut his fist, making no move to clasp Mum's hand in return. It was lovely that Mum was making the overtures, but an attendant came along and spoiled the moment.

My thoughts drifted back to what we had left. Our house and all our possessions had gone, taking with them our history, at least in the form of things you could touch, hold and examine. All we had now were memories. We didn't even have friends any more. Friends are dangerous.

On the ground too, what was happening? The Gorgon's men – what were they up to? What did they know, and what were they already reporting to the man who paid them?

Although I'd never met the man, I'd formed an impression of someone who looked fatherly and thoroughly respectable – not ugly, as my sister's nickname for him suggested. Maybe, as we nervously raced in police cars across England, he'd been having a few business acquaintances in for dinner. It would have been a date he'd arranged before he was taken into custody, that he'd refuse to cancel. He'd want to show the world how normal he was, how respectable.

Towards the end of the meal, as his wife poured

coffee, maybe the phone would ring. He'd rise to answer it, perhaps taking his glass of brandy with him. His caller would say, 'They're leaving from Stanstead.'

'Find out where they're off to,' the Gorgon would say, before hanging up and going back to his guests.

'Who was that, dear?' his wife might ask.

'Just business,' he'd answer, and he'd pour himself more brandy. She'd know not to press the matter.

It was unlikely, I thought, that anyone on this charter aircraft to Australia would have Gorgon connections. All the same, I found myself scanning any face that passed along the aisle.

We accepted some airline food, after which we settled to sleep. The kilometres peeled off, putting distance between us and the hateful cause of our anxiety.

People tell traveller's tales of horror flights. Ours was just long, uncomfortable and boring, with narrow seats and little leg room. This aircraft had been fitted out for short journeys, not for going halfway around the world. There was no inflight entertainment, and no magazines in the seat pocket – nor did the attendants offer any. None of us had even considered bringing a book, so the hours were tedious. All you could do was think.

The first stop was Calcutta, where we landed on a hot, hazy afternoon, with a spicy fragrance in the air. We had to endure a lengthy delay – a problem over refuelling the aircraft, someone said. At first they wouldn't let any of us off, but after an hour they relented. We all trooped sweatily into the terminal building, where we sat around in a roped off section marked 'Transit Passengers'.

None of us were dressed for the tropics. Nicola and I wore woollen skirts and sweaters, which we couldn't very well take off. We had started out wearing tights, which we discarded some time before we landed at Calcutta, but even so it was uncomfortably hot and sticky, making me long for a bath or a shower and change of clothes. It was annoying to think that there was an air-conditioned part of this airport, where we could have gone shopping – perhaps to buy T-shirts or even saris! Incongruous, but cooler. As it was, we sweated in this heat, which made me remember how it would have been at home right now. Our real home.

Through the terminal window we could see our aircraft in the hazy distance, but there was no sign of a fuel truck. Some of our fellow passengers were Australians who'd been living and working in Britain. Nicola and I edged closer, because they were the only ones who accepted the delay with good humour. There were men and women, some of them not much older than me. I took note of that!

By this time Mum and Dad were more at ease, and didn't mind us stretching our legs in this way.

The Australians were laughing and joking. There was one particular couple that caught my eye. They sat together, he with his arm casually around her shoulder and she leaning in towards him, with both hands on his knee. Seeing them like that, I felt a great sense of longing. Okay, I've had it before – so it's nothing new – but suddenly I had this desire to be like them.

'What do you reckon,' I heard one of the Australians say. 'Think they still owe money for fuel – '

'What, from last time they were through here?'

'Yeah. Bet the skipper's cheque bounced and they've impounded the aircraft.'

'So when's the next train?' another of them asked, and they started to sing, *Oh why are we waiting*? The girl joined in, which is when Mum called us away.

At last a fuel truck rolled slowly out to the plane, but no one seemed to be in any hurry. Maybe the fuel company *was* waiting for the captain's cheque to clear. I once heard a story of a situation like this, where the fuel company wouldn't deliver. At last, one of the flight attendants bought the fuel on her American Express card. I bet she was worried!

'Where exactly are we going, Dad?' Nicola asked. In all this time, we hadn't thought to ask that question. Australia was Australia, so we imagined we'd just end up somewhere like Ramsay Street from *Neighbours*.

'Brisbane,' Dad answered. 'We'll stay in your grand-mother's old house in Raglan Street.' As a name, it was pretty close to Ramsay Street, and as we'd seen photos of Gran's house, we already knew something about the place. That was a plus.

Gran was dead now – about five or six years ago, and Dad had had to go over for the funeral. Once, when I was five and Nicola just three years old, she had come to Manchester for a visit, but my memories of her are very vague. Dad had always wanted to take us all out to meet her girls, but it was not to be. The only real knowledge we'd had of her were the letters she'd sent every fortnight, from time to time including photos of herself, or of the house and garden, each with Gran's elegant handwriting on the back.

But those letters and pictures were now no more – lost in the fire.

They called us to board the stifling aircraft, and we took off. No word of explanation for the hold-up, but once we were airborne it became cooler, and the food was nice. So I've been to Calcutta, but for all I saw of the place it might have been Wigan, Glasgow or Bolton.

There is nothing to say about the rest of the flight – apart from another long delay in Hong Kong, where the aircraft was parked well away from the terminal. We could see the big prestige airliners when we drove past on the transit bus – Lufthansa, KLM, Qantas, Singapore Airlines, Cathay Pacific. Our aircraft had no name at all. Anonymous Airlines, Nicola called it. I overheard an attendant tell a passenger that they were delivering the plane to someone in the Pacific Islands. Maybe it was some fabulously wealthy rock star who'd bought it. Perhaps he'd paint it vivid colours and give it a really stupid name. I hoped he'd be airsick!

In the Hong Kong terminal I managed to buy a paperback, but it was really depressing. Then we flew on to Darwin, for another delay, and finally into Brisbane, where we landed at 0500 on a hot cloudless December morning, with the sun already climbing in the sky. Again they parked our aircraft well away from the terminal building. We had to walk, with stern-looking officials keeping an eye on us in case we might wander off. They wore unfriendly sunglasses.

When they got off, a couple of the young Australians dropped to their knees and kissed the tarmac. As they followed behind us, one of them started reciting some kind of patriotic poem, and they all ended up saying the last verse which was, 'God bless Australia!' I saw Dad grinning at this. After such a flight, how could they manage to keep a sense of humour?

'Look at the sky, Emma,' Nicola called back to me. She had marched ahead of us, bubbling with excitement – another person with boundless optimism. 'Look at the sky.'

'What's wrong with it?' I asked.

'It's away up there. Look.' It sounded silly, but it was true. The sky seemed to be limitless, the deepest blue, with not a cloud in sight. In Manchester, especially on a rainy grey day, the sky seemed to be just above your head, but here, I had an amazing feeling of space.

As we got closer to the terminal, one of the officials remarked, 'She's gonna be a scorcher.'

'Yeah,' his mate answered. 'Gonna be more rain though.'

'Yeah, we need it.' As they spoke, neither of them appeared to open their mouths. Like ventriloquists.

The immigration people seemed to know about Mum, Dad and our situation, for the formalities were soon over. We wheeled our bags out, facing a throng of people who were waiting to greet incoming passengers from Singapore. None of them were meeting us, so we eased past with our luggage trolley.

There was so much colour. Everyone seemed to be in shorts and sandals. Girls wore brief tops or T-shirts, looking cool and crisp. In my sturdy British winter gear I felt like some kind of Eskimo.

The young Australians from our flight emerged from the customs section, and a great cheer went up from a group of people in the crowd.

'You mean there are more of them?' Mum asked.

''Fraid so, Lil,' Dad said, but he was grinning. Outside, in the humid morning air, we queued for a taxi. My sweater was hot against my skin, so I pulled the neck and gave it a shake. Perspiration was the order of the day.

I felt a sudden slap between my shoulder blades as something landed there, a heavy thing. I reached over to dislodge it, but my arm wasn't long enough. What was I doing? Reaching out to touch this – whatever it was!

'Dad, what's on me?' I turned my back to show him.

'Oh yes.' Dad took the thing off and hid it in his hand. He had a half-smile on his face as he released whatever it was. With a whirring, clicking sound, the thing flapped away.

'Dad, what was it?'

'Only a grasshopper, Emma.'

'Oh, I wanted to see that,' Nicola protested. 'Why'd you let it go, Dad?'

'Plenty more where he came from,' Dad assured her.

'But it was as big as a sparrow.' My voice was weak. 'Nearly knocked me over.'

Further back in the queue, a man was laughing. 'Welcome to Australia,' he said.

Then it was our turn for a taxi. It wasn't air-conditioned, so we wound the windows down and let the warm breeze play on our faces.

'She's gonna be a scorcher, folks,' the driver told us. He wore shorts and had hairy legs. His radio was on, and the announcer confirmed his words: '*A fine day in the city, heading for a top of thirty-three, thirty-six in Ipswich, and tonight we're in for a thunderstorm.*' Then came some Christmassy music that made me think of our Timperley home. At this time of year, it was always dark when we got home in the afternoon. Nicola and I would help Mum put up our own decorations. We'd erect the tree and untangle the fairy lights, then we'd adorn the branches until they drooped with the weight. I thought of Sandra and the girls at school. They'd be decorating the classroom, looking forward to the holidays, which would be starting about now. I was glad no one spoke to me just then.

Seeing our new city was exciting, but depressing too in a way. The buildings were so different. I felt like an alien. Yes, this was my new home, but to be familiar with it, I'd have to know where all these buses were going –

Salisbury, Mt Gravatt, Toombul. Then I'd need to make friends. As we drove through the streets, the list of things to do just kept growing, like some kind of huge, daunting project.

The city was bright, colourful and clean – so different from Manchester. Buildings sparkled white in the morning sun, and some seemed to be made of blue-tinted glass. We'd hit the morning rush-hour, the driver told us, explaining why it took so long. People in the streets wore sunglasses and hats and light clothes – they were going to work looking as if they were on holiday. Soon we were through the city and into a suburb. We reached the top of a hill. Below us was a sea of red-roofed houses – all with people in them, I supposed, going about their cheerful Christmas business without having to look over their shoulders.

But at least out here we'd be free of that too. Come on, I told myself, this is why we came, to be free of apprehension. I brightened. All the precautions the police took, surely they had to count for something?

Raglan Street was pretty enough, with a canopy of orange-coloured poinciana trees spreading shade along its entire length. It was very quiet. There weren't any people in the street. Maybe they were all indoors, away from the rising heat. Most of the houses stood alone on big blocks of land, and there were trees in everyone's garden, with some of the most vivid flowers you could imagine – reds, purples and yellows.

'Don't know what state the place will be in,' Dad said, as we drew up at Number 34. 'We've had tenants living in it.'

'Tenants?' the driver echoed. 'Don't talk to me about tenants.' He got out to help us with the bags. 'Twenty-seven dollars,' he said to Dad, who gave him some notes. 'And three change. Have a happy Christmas, folks.' He waved cheerfully then drove away.

'You didn't give him a tip, Dad,' Nicola said. She watches everything.

'Funny that,' Dad answered. His face became serious as he picked up two of our bags.

Mum bit her lip as she surveyed the house. 'I just feel,' she started to say. 'I feel this is day one and there's been nothing before it – we've no history, no – '

'Yeah,' Dad agreed, and pushed the gate open.

But they were wrong. We had a neighbour. She'd been weeding the shrubs at her front fence when we arrived, but now she stood up, took off her gloves, and came over to us.

She was old, about sixty or so, maybe older. Even *she* wore shorts and a T-shirt, plus a baseball cap with a name on it. *Yankees*, it said. Her skin was tanned, and she had a half-smile of recognition on her face.

'It's Don, isn't it? Don Cassidy?' She used our real surname, and Dad didn't correct her. Instead, he greeted her warmly.

'Mrs Stone? You're still living here?'

'You mean, am I still living?' she said. Dad introduced us to Mrs Stone, who'd lived next-door for years, watched Dad grow up, *that* sort of neighbour. 'Wish you'd said you were coming,' she went on. 'Could have got some things in for you.'

'We'll manage.' Dad left Mrs Stone and went up the path to the house. It had a verandah.

'Kept an eye on the place.' Mrs Stone started weeding again. 'Tenants weren't too bad. Only moved out last week.'

'Yes.' Dad produced a set of keys from an electrical meter box, opened the front door, and ushered us across the threshold.

The house wasn't like any in Ramsay Street.

Number 34 Raglan Street was an old timber house with a dark central living room, a high ceiling, and a polished wooden floor. Inside it was hot and musty, so we ran around opening all the windows, letting in heavy flower smells from the garden, as well as the chirruping noise that I later recognised as the sound of a Brisbane summer – crickets.

'Smell that bush,' Dad said. 'That's Australia. Coming back, it really hits you.' Wilting with the heat, none of us shared his enthusiasm.

'A cup of tea would be nice,' Mum said weakly.

'And a bath,' I added.

We took stock. This house was even worse than the one we had back in Illingworth. At least that had been newish. This one was old, with a drab look about it, and all the time I had this sticky, grubby feeling. My priority

107

was a bath, then some fresh, cool clothes. As I stood in one of the bedrooms, the one that would be mine, Nicola came in from the adjoining room. (There was a door between them.)

'Here we go again.' She sat on the bed. 'Gets worse and worse. But at least we're safe.' Dad came into the room, forcing the cheerfulness, I thought.

'Come on, girls, give me a smile.'

'Yes, Dad.' Nicola showed her teeth, but I wasn't in the mood.

'Look, it'll take a bit of time for us to find our feet,' Dad went on. 'I've switched on the hot water, so you can unpack, have a shower, then get into some cooler clothes, eh?'

'Yes, okay Dad,' we answered automatically.

'And, um – ' he hesitated. 'Even here we need to be watchful.' Nicola and I just sighed.

The shower was tingly cold, and fresh – but in the cool clothes department, there was a snag. When Mum packed for me in our Timperley house, she'd packed winter things – after all, she thought we'd need them, and had fondly imagined we'd collect the rest of our things later. The clothes we'd brought from England were not what you'd call cool.

As I dressed in the lightest gear I possessed, there came a call from the front door, which Dad had left open for ventilation.

'Yoo, hoo! Only me.' It was Mrs Stone.

'Huh,' Nicola muttered. 'Next-door Nosey Mark Two.'

'Shh, she'll hear you,' I warned.

Mrs Stone carried a tray, bearing a large teapot, some cups, milk, and something she'd baked, which was wrapped in a tea-towel.

'Soon as I saw you,' she said, 'I thought, now there go some folk who could do with a cuppa.'

Since there was no refusing, we reluctantly gathered in the living room. Mrs Stone was no-nonsense about it, setting out the cups on a low table, showing us the thing she'd baked – a sort of crusty loaf with fruit in it, which brought a smile of recognition to Dad's face.

'Damper.' He sniffed the warm odour appreciatively, while Mrs Stone urged us to eat and drink.

The Brisbane water gave the tea a funny taste, but Mrs Stone assured us that after two cups we'd love it.

'You could have given me a ring from Manchester or wherever,' she went on. 'I could have aired the place, brought you fresh linen.'

'We made up our minds in a hurry,' Dad told her.

'And what fetched you back?' Mrs Stone wasn't like Next-door Nosey – she assumed a *right* to question us. After all, she'd known Dad for years.

'A new job,' Mum said. 'It just came up.' Dad nodded.

'So we gave the tenants notice – '

'They were already going,' Mrs Stone interrupted. 'Built their own place. Away out beyond Strathpine.'

'Away out there?' Dad marvelled at the news, and took a slice of damper.

Mrs Stone owned a car, a 1975-model Holden, which she rarely used since her husband had died, preferring to go everywhere by bike or on the bus. So Dad borrowed the Holden, and took us on an emergency buying spree for groceries, bed linen, shorts, T-shirts and sandals.

'When they see our white legs, they'll need sunglasses,' Nicola huffed.

'No one tans these days,' Dad informed her – white was all right, as the slogan went. But even so, we stood out in that air-conditioned shopping centre, which was another riot of colourful clothing. I found myself envying some girls my age, who managed to look cool despite the heat of the day. If it were left to me, I'd just move into a shopping centre and live there – after all, there was everything you'd need!

We drove home with our boot filled with plastic bags. Mrs Stone had urged us to leave the house open to air and, what with us being a whole lot fresher and more cheerful, the house seemed to be cooler inside, and the musty odour had gone. We unloaded the car, then set about making the place fit to live in.

Mrs Stone came around to see how we were coping, and to give us some news – innocent enough for her but ominous for us.

'There was a man looking for you,' she said.

I shuddered in sudden fear, which Mrs Stone noticed. She frowned.

'You all right, Emma?'

'Yes,' I lied. 'It's just this heat – '

'And the long journey,' Mum came to my aid. 'We're all jet-lagged.'

'Well, I'll let you settle in.' Mrs Stone went off. Then, pausing at the front door, 'Oh, there's going to be a bit of rain tonight, so make sure you fasten your windows.'

When she'd gone, we appealed to Dad. Who was the man? Did it mean –

'Relax,' he said. 'I couldn't tell you in front of Mrs Stone.' Dad had been expecting a visit from an Australian Federal Police liaison officer.

On our first night in Australia, the darkness arrived – just like that. It was light, then it was dark. If anything, the crickets became even louder, their noise almost reaching a constant scream. It stayed oppressively hot. But now Nicola and I were dressed for the heat in our K-Mart T-shirts and shorts, so we thought we were going to beat this thing.

'It'll be cooler soon,' Dad told us.

'When?' I demanded. 'March or April?'

In my narrow bed, I tossed and turned, kicked the top sheet off, and lay, still sweltering. From their restless movements, I could tell the others had similar problems.

'We'll get fans tomorrow,' Dad bellowed.

'Air-conditioning,' Nicola shouted back. Then came a zinging noise in my ear, reminding me that we'd forgotten to buy mosquito repellent!

At last it became too much for me. I felt my upper lip swell, dashed to the bathroom, and snapped on the light to stare at a puffy, swollen face in the mirror. My eyes were almost closed. I thought of the gentle boy on the morning bus in Timperley. He wouldn't even recognise me now. No one would. Nicola came to join me in the bathroom. She too had attracted the mosquitoes.

'Shove over,' she said ungraciously, then slumped dismally when she saw the meat-red mess that confronted her.

'Looking like that,' I told her, 'you'll be a spinster till you die.' Before she could reply, there came a huge flash of lightning, which lit up the house, followed by the mightiest, rolling clap of thunder that I'd ever heard. It reverberated away, and away, over the suburbs.

A gentle, cooling breeze stirred the curtains.

7

The breeze became stronger. Soon there was also a distant hissing noise and, further away, the rumble of thunder. Nicola and I forgot our mosquito-raddled faces and enjoyed the cool that came with the breeze. But as the wind picked up and the hissing grew louder, we became alarmed. Then, Dad was on the scene, with Mum not far behind.

'Come on, girls, close all the windows.' Dad took charge. 'Storm coming.' He moved off, leaving us to our fate.

We'd closed three of the bedroom windows before the rain started splatting down. The single heavy droplets landed with a series of smacks on some broad-leaved plant in the garden. With a whistling sound, the wind gathered force. Then the rain began to fall in earnest, and soon became an almost impenetrable sheet, dropping vertically from the sky. If you got caught out in so much falling water, I wondered, could you possibly breathe?

The torrent was accompanied by an almost continuous series of lightning flashes, followed by rolling peals of thunder, which made the walls of our bedrooms shake.

The rain on the corrugated-iron roof created a noise so loud we were unable to hear each other speak. Nicola and I just stood as all this happened around us.

Dad tried to shout something to us, but the din made it impossible to hear. He had a grin on his face, as if he'd put on this show for our benefit. Then the lights went out, leaving us with nothing but the occasional lightning flash to see by. It was a horrible feeling, not being able to see or hear. Anyone could have entered the house and wandered around.

The storm lasted another ten minutes, then the rain lessened into a steady downpour, and the lightning moved away from us, taking its grumbling thunder with it. We could make ourselves heard at last, but the lights stayed off. Apart from the fright, it had been impressive.

'You can open the windows again, girls,' Dad told us. 'Be a bit cooler, too.' He was still grinning, but Mum hadn't enjoyed the experience. She came from her bedroom, and we met in the kitchen.

'You never mentioned this, Don,' she said.

'Yes,' I demanded of my father. 'How often does it happen?'

'Summer's the time for them,' Dad told us. 'But wait till you get hailstorms too, they're really impressive, especially in the daytime. The sky turns dark green then down they come – hailstones as big as golf balls. Cricket balls.' Dad was getting carried away.

Eventually, the rain stopped altogether, and the sound of crickets crept back in. The night air was cooler, but as we crawled back into bed, the mosquitoes went on the rampage once more.

In the morning, with my face still puffy, I got up, detesting the place and all its torments with a passion. It was as if I'd been promised something, only to find it was all a sham. This wasn't like *Neighbours*. I felt let down. My homesickness was at its peak.

Mum and Dad were still in bed. I went out front to the verandah, expecting to see, after such a storm, the neighbouring houses flattened, flooding, people needing rescuing, ambulances even. But nothing was out of place – the street was wet, but the sun was already high in the sky, and birds sang.

Mrs Stone came past from her house, wearing a large white bicycle helmet and wheeling her bike. She saw me and smiled.

'Hullo, Emmy,' she said. 'Nice drop of rain last night.' A nice drop of rain? It was a solid wall of water, it was a hurricane, a cyclone, a tempest, a cloudburst. Submarines could have navigated their way through it – and Mrs Stone calls it a nice drop of rain. She paused at our front gate, and saw my swollen face. 'Oh, I should have warned you about the mossies.' She spoke regretfully, as if she'd let us down. 'Fresh out from the old country, they'd just love you. You and your sister need to get yourselves coils.' She mounted her bicycle. 'I'm off to get my *Courier-Mail*, Emmy. Hoo-roo.'

'Hoo-roo,' I answered automatically. I'd have to work

on that Emmy bit. But getting myself a coil? It sounded vaguely contraceptive, and later when I reported as much to Mum at the breakfast table, Dad almost choked into his cereal bowl. It was the first time I'd seen Mum laugh since we arrived.

Nicola, barefoot and still in her cotton nightgown, had already gone to explore the jungle at the back. I went down the wooden stairs to join her.

From the back garden, I could see that the house was supported on tall timber stilts. The land sloped away sharply, so that the front of the house was at street level, while the back was high off the ground. There was a large cool space underneath, where you could hang washing on wet days. The mosquitoes started on my bare ankles.

'It stands on stilts,' I remarked to Nicola, slapping at my calves.

'Dad said people here call them stumps,' she told me. 'Makes the house cool.'

'Not that I noticed,' I said.

There was a shed at the bottom of the garden, but the door was off its hinges, and it looked a dark place, wrangled in thorny weeds and probably full of huge insects. The garden backed on to a thick grove of gum trees – some kind of forest park, Dad told us. I remembered, from the colourful photos Gran sent, that she was very proud of her garden. Nicola, it seemed, was the one to inherit that satisfaction.

'Birds, butterflies, everything,' she bubbled. 'You'll love it, Emma.'

'We get enough wildlife inside,' I told her and, with a

final slap at my ankle, ran upstairs to find something to eat.

After breakfast, a man came. He identified himself as a federal police officer, then he and Dad went off to the front verandah to have a talk, leaving Mum and me in the kitchen.

'Well, what do you think, Mum?' I asked. It was the first chance that we'd had to talk. Mum shrugged helplessly.

'It's all a bit – ' she looked around the kitchen, which was decidedly old-fashioned and dowdy compared with home. 'It's all a bit too much to take in.'

'I know what you mean,' I said. 'I keep thinking of – '

'Yes.' She cut me off, then made an effort to brighten. 'Still, we're here now, and we'll just have to get on with it.'

Dad came back from the verandah, but he wouldn't be drawn about what they had been discussing. It was as if he was shielding us – he had caused it, so he'd handle it.

By mid-morning our puffiness had subsided, so we set out again, courtesy of Mrs Stone's car. The shopping-centre was only a couple of kilometres away. It was surrounded by street after street of houses. Most of them weren't as pretty as ours, and they seemed to be crowded closer together. There were no flowering trees shading the length of these streets.

It wasn't until we were inside the cool of the shopping-centre that I paused and smiled, realising that I'd had a good thought about Raglan Street.

We bought electric fans and a whole arsenal of mosquito defence equipment. Armed with this lot, we could spray, zap and smoke the entire insect world into submission. It would probably be the end of us too, but that's the price you pay. I wished we could do the same with Mr You-Know-Who back in Manchester.

The Christmas spirit was everywhere. With great determination we joined the spending spree, buying a plastic tree and things to deck the walls of our house. We still had time to think about presents for each other, but we wouldn't need to worry about Christmas cards. If none of this had happened, Mum and Dad would have sent their cards long ago. Nicola and I would have added our bit to the pile of seasonal good wishes that fanned out from the Cassidy family, but this year there would be nothing like that. No cards would come and none would go.

What about all the people back home who wouldn't get one from us? I wondered. And the people who'd ring us up over Christmas?

'That's strange,' they'd say. 'Their phone's been disconnected.' And maybe if one or two of them chanced to drop in at the old house, they'd find the reason – but they'd have no idea where to make inquiries about us. The neighbours wouldn't know.

These were bleak thoughts amid all the shopping-centre cheer. I looked at girls my age who didn't have to worry about stuff like this. They all seemed so carefree, in their giggling groups, having fun. I envied them.

118

Dad bought another mobile phone, as his British one had actually belonged to the police. There was a phone at the Raglan Street house, which had to be re-connected, at more expense. Not that it ever rang, unlike the old days at home, when it was sometimes impossible to prise Nicola away from the earpiece. To make us even more remote, this phone had an unlisted number.

As he had promised, Dad made contact with the Man-chester CID to give them our phone number and a pro-gress report. The Australian Federal Police officer had been brief, leaving emergency numbers for himself and for the Brisbane CIB, who already knew about us. Another plain-clothes policeman came one day with an answering machine, which he attached to the phone line.

'Never answer right away,' he advised us. 'Let the machine take the call and if it's one of us or someone you know, you can interrupt.' There was a recorded message, a woman's voice, which just gave our number and told the caller to leave a message. 'There's a lot of other safety precautions you must take,' the policeman went on.

The precautions spelled out a few grim facts of our new life. We had to acquire a post office box for our mail, and we mustn't have any deliveries made to the house – milk, newspapers, that sort of thing. We were never to allow any tradespeople inside unless we had checked their IDs. We were to record descriptions, name and car number if possible, of anyone who came to the house, for whatever reason. For the time being, Nicola and I were to confine our outings to family ones – no romantic dates, not that there were any on the horizon, no movies or rock concerts unless our folks came too. Fat chance!

We were also told to be suspicious of any parcels that were delivered, and generally to keep an eye open for strangers watching the house, people following us, or anything at all out of place. No matter how trivial it seemed, we were to ring one of our emergency numbers and report it.

When he was ready to leave, the policeman and Dad walked out to the verandah, where Nicola and I had found a shady spot to read.

'If there's anything more, Mr Morton, don't hesitate to ring.'

'Will do,' Dad agreed.

Mrs Stone was waiting at the front gate, and smiled as the policeman passed her on the way to his car.

'I'm off to my sister's, Don,' she announced. 'Wondered if you'd water my pot-plants. That's if you're staying put for Christmas.'

'Yes, we'll be here,' Dad told her. They talked about which plants and where, then Mrs Stone suddenly launched a surprise attack.

'Don, that fellow called you Mr Morton.'

'Um – yes,' Dad agreed. Mrs Stone shrugged, then half closed one eye.

'So how does that come about?'

I could almost see Dad thinking on his feet. This one had really thrown him.

'Um – I took my wife's name,' he said.

'English custom, is it?'

'M-mm.' Dad nodded, then spoke more decisively. 'So these days we're the Morton family.' Inwardly, I cheered my father for handling the situation so neatly. Then after a few more words of conversation, Mrs Stone left. I could see from her manner that Dad's stature had somehow been diminished. But not with us. As he walked back into the house, he caught our eyes and gave a slight, embarrassed shrug.

'Nice one, Dad,' Nicola said with a wink.

In the days that led up to Christmas, it stayed hot. Temperatures were in the low thirties or high twenties, with high humidity. We had more rain, but nothing as fierce as the storm of the first night. The weather seemed to be a major preoccupation here.

Nicola was in love with the back garden. Entomologist, zoologist and now ornithologist, for the birds came around in swarms, and in such variety. There was a bird-feeding table, on which Dad scattered handfuls of seed he'd bought at the supermarket. Well, it made sense. You plant seed, and get flowers. Spread a different kind, and you get birds, which can be just as pretty.

Nicola was soon identifying them – lorikeets, king parrots, a galah or two, and even a huge cockatoo. In our part of the world, you'd have to visit Chester Zoo to see birds like them. I pretended to be grudging in my admiration, but they were beautiful all the same, especially the lorikeets – small, cheerful birds, that somehow reminded me of the Australians who'd travelled with us.

We took photos of the birds, but we didn't discuss who we'd share them with. I'd love to have sent them to Sandra, especially the one that Nicola took of me standing really close to the feeding table, with some of my rainbow lorikeets gorging away quite unconcerned. *Cop this, Sandra*! I'd have written on the back.

With Mrs Stone away, we had the place to ourselves. Such a strange Christmas dinner, with us barefoot in shorts and the outside temperature hovering around thirty-three degrees. We had a turkey and all of the usual things, but although we did our best, it was just not the thing to be eating in the middle of the day so one by one, we pushed our plates away.

'Salad's the thing,' Dad said. 'Seafood and salad.' We had a go at the plum pudding, but eventually it joined the turkey leftovers in the bin.

We sat around our tree, solemnly passing each other presents which we'd secretly bought, not an easy thing to do when you're under constant surveillance. As we unwrapped our gifts I could tell everyone was thinking of home, and what we'd been doing this time last year. I remember we had carols on Christmas Eve, and we all rugged up and went for our traditional walk after Christmas lunch. It was cold and truly Christmassy.

At that moment, more perhaps than at any other time, I felt how foreign our whole situation was. Normally, spending Christmas in Australia would have been the most fantastic adventure, but not like this, not *having* to be here.

Poor Dad did his best to cheer us up. He had a family present, a large envelope which Mum opened. It contained a glossy brochure featuring our new car, a Ford Falcon, which we'd take delivery of after Christmas. And yes, it was air-conditioned. The insurance on our house and effects had come through, so we could afford a few things, and at least with a car we could go places. We all brightened up.

'It's not a Beamer,' I said. 'But it'll do.'

'Nor is it Daimler,' Nicola added, then she put the brochure down, got up from the floor, and went to her room.

Mum and Dad both had Queensland licenses now, so Mum insisted on driving as much as possible. Poor Dad would normally have made excuses as to why he should drive, but maybe he saw it as a way of taking Mum's mind off things.

It was several days after Christmas. We were on a country road, with Mum at the wheel, bowling along quite smoothly towards Mount Tamborine, which was the place I'd chosen for this outing. (We all took turns, using an RACQ roadmap to pick our destination.) All was going well. The car was comfortable and cool. Then I noticed Mum's eyes in the rear-view mirror. She looked apprehensive.

I glanced out of the back window to see a much older car trailing along behind us, right on our tail, with barely a vehicle length between us. The car was an iridescent purple colour with chrome decorations, and even from inside our car, I could hear the roar of its engine.

'Well, come on, pass if you must,' Mum muttered. This alerted Dad to the situation.

'What's wrong, Lil?'

'This idiot's been on my tail since the turn-off back there.'

'Pull over,' Dad suggested.

'The road's clear. He can pass.' Mum flicked the indicator and eased to the left. The other car overtook, but then slowed down to drive alongside us. The front passenger, a man with dark hair and sunglasses, leaned out and stared at us, all the while chewing gum. I couldn't see the driver properly.

This is it, I remember thinking. They've found us.

Mum slowed our car to a stop. The other vehicle drifted slowly on along the road, as if the driver was undecided about whether to do something. I must admit to a feeling of panic but then, thankfully, a large truck came from behind. There was a hiss of brakes, then the truck driver sounded an angry blast on his airhorn. The other car took off, with a roar of exhaust.

'I'm shaking,' Mum said.

'Want me to drive?' Dad offered.

'I can manage,' Mum snapped. 'I simply don't like being – ' She didn't finish her sentence.

'Just a bunch of hoons,' Dad said. 'We get them in Britain. Yobs.'

'I got his number,' Nicola spoke up.

'Well, we'll report them,' Mum said firmly. If it had

happened to anyone else who was out for a relaxing drive that afternoon, it might have passed with no more than angry words. The hoons hadn't done anything, apart from drive too closely behind us then stare at us. But after what we'd been through, the incident was deeply disturbing. When Mum finally drove on, we were all reduced to silence.

We stopped at Tamborine Village, a pretty little mountain place, with houses set well back from the road and some unusual-looking shops. There was only one main street, which had a serene, sort of sleepy afternoon air about it. Dad said he'd shout us tea.

'Tea!' Nicola shouted. 'There you are, Dad. I shouted tea too.' She's such a humorist, my sister. Dad patiently explained the meaning of 'shout', as in to treat. An important verb to know if we were to blend in with the natives, Nicola told him gravely.

We relaxed in a little teashop, next-door to one of those hotels that sold XXXX. When she'd eaten, Nicola excused herself and went around the back to the toilet. When she returned, we gathered ourselves for the trip home.

Dad took the wheel this time, saying there were some tricky downhill curves to be negotiated. Mum gave him an arch look. We were laughing now – it was all so relaxed and, well, family.

The car was a blessing. Our situation had been getting to Mum more and more, causing her to draw into her shell. There was just nothing to do and, as someone who'd had such an active life, Mum had been

125

feeling it more than the rest of us. They say that when professional women like architects and doctors have babies, they suffer post-natal depression more than most women. It's the sudden loss of a stimulating professional life that does it – being cooped up with a baby all the time.

So it must have been like that for Mum: friendless, no one to confide in, not able to go anywhere on her own. And having to be alert, in a way she'd never had to be before. So the car made a big change by allowing us to get away from the house, which was depressing us.

On the way down Mount Tamborine, Nicola was in the back with Mum, and I sat with Dad in the front. We'd hardly gone a kilometre before Nicola handed Mum something.

'A present for you, Mummy,' she said quietly.

'What are these, Nicola?' Mum was mystified by the things in her palm.

'They're something to do with tyres,' Nicola told her. 'They hold the air in.' Dad frowned. He pulled into the side of the road, and turned around.

'Valve cores.' He recognised the things.

'I found the hoons' car,' Nicola said simply. 'It was in the pub car park – '

'And you let the air out of their tyres?' Dad was suddenly angry. 'Look, with their type, you let well alone.'

Nicola was defensive. 'I couldn't resist it. Anyway, nobody saw me. Besides, one bad turn – '

Dad almost exploded. 'Don't – don't – ' He couldn't find a word.

'Don't be provocative, Nicola.' Mum finished the sentence that Dad couldn't get out.

'Turn the other cheek?' Nicola folded her arms. 'That's our role in life?' Dad gave a signal, then drove on.

'It's all we can do,' Mum explained gently, but Nicola insisted on the last word.

'Wouldn't we like to get back at the Gorgon?'

Dad didn't answer. He concentrated on a bend in the road. Nicola took the valve cores from Mum, and held two of them to her ears. 'They'd make nice earrings, Emma,' she said. 'Want a pair?'

I took two of the valve cores, and held them in my palm all the way back to Raglan Street. A week later, I had lost mine, but when I went into Nicola's room, I found she'd tied her pair with red cotton and hung them at the side of her mirror, as if they were a trophy.

I wished then I'd kept mine too.

There were enormous spiders in the house – huntsmen, Dad called them. They were really huge, and they'd sort of lurk in dark places, then scuttle out to race up the wall. They always ran away, which was a good thing, but their size made me shiver. Nicola, budding entomologist, would go close and examine the spiders with a magnifying glass.

'They're more afraid than you are,' she told me.

'How can you possibly know?'

We had managed to quell the mosquitoes, but there

were other examples of wildlife that regarded our home as theirs – we had green tree frogs who lived in the toilet, and had to be encouraged outside. Dad wouldn't let us touch them, because secretions from our skin could harm them. Well, excuse me, Mister Frog. Pardon me for breathing!

Sometimes, horror of horrors, a frog or toad got into my room at night and I had to call for Nicola.

'Huh,' she snorted, as she dealt with the beast. 'From now on, the charge is fifty cents up to midnight, after that a dollar.' Which was another thing. Nicola became familiar with dollars and cents long before I did. I still talked about pounds and pence.

'It was forty p,' I'd say, and Nicola would automatically correct me.

'She means cents.'

When it rained we hung our laundry under the house. That area was infested with large, warty toads, so if Mum asked me to get something off the clothes line after dark, I refused – wisely as it turned out, for one night something happened that we'll never forget.

Nicola, who thought herself to be Miss Wildlife personified, seemed unconcerned about toads, frogs and the very small lizards that were everywhere, sunning themselves in the daytime. Just to show how bold she was, one night she went downstairs to get something off the line, including some items that belonged to me.

From upstairs I heard her humming to herself, then she talked to a toad, which she often did, saying things

128

like, 'Hello, Mr Toad, how are things in Toad Hall? How are Mole and Ratty?'

This night, she said, 'Come on, Mr Toad, shove off.' Sometimes, to show how much at one she was with nature, she'd use her bare foot to clear a toad out of her way, which she'd obviously done on this occasion. Then her voice changed. 'Help,' she called, in a very small voice. 'Somebody, help!'

Dad and Mum went downstairs, to find her standing under the single light bulb, almost frozen to the spot, looking at an armful of my clothes that she'd thrown on the ground. I viewed all of this from the top of the stairs.

'Under there,' Nicola said. 'I pushed it with my foot. Not a toad.' She was petrified. The pile of clothes moved. Dad got closer and flicked the top garment away. It was a snake, curled up so we couldn't estimate its length.

'Python,' Dad informed us. He seemed in no haste to kill it or shift it from the clothes. Nor did the snake seem to be in a hurry to move off. From where I stood I could see its tongue flickering, as it considered us and we regarded it. 'It won't harm you,' Dad went on. 'It can bite, but it's not poisonous.'

He knelt near the snake, and looked at it until Mum ventured closer. Nicola followed, so of course I had to go down too. We all crowded around to look at the thing. As Dad pointed out, it was quite beautifully marked. Eventually, and without hurrying, it slid away into the darkness. Nicola gathered my clothes and we went back upstairs.

'A metre-and-a-half,' Dad said.

I wandered around with a feeling of smugness, me being at one with the wildlife, having stood close to a real live snake and not thrown a panic attack. Then Dad spoiled it by telling us that when he was a boy, snakes used to come into the house. On one occasion, he'd found one curled in his bed. If they could come in then, my reasoning went, they could come in now.

There was always something or other that would send me off in fright. If there's anything in this reincarnation business, then I promise not to be the wimpy one of the family – next time we come back.

There were other wildlife events, such as the large grey lizard that I thought was a bit of wood. Ha, ha. Then came the invasion of the fruit-bats. They arrived unannounced in the trees outside my bedroom, screeching and making an unearthly flap with their wings. At any second, I expected to see one of them land on my windowsill, wearing a dinner suit and an opera cape!

But gradually, as January wore on, I became more and more used to the place and, in a way, I began to find it beautiful. The thing about coming to Australia is that the type of beauty that you're used to in Britain just isn't here. In Britain there are greener greens, and more distinct seasons, with something beautiful in each of them – the starkness of a leafless tree silhouetted against a misty background, the colours of autumn. Whereas in Australia the air seemed to be clearer, and the colours sharper, with much more variety. With everything else, you have to become acclimatised – so I suppose it's the same with beauty.

The lifestyle was definitely relaxed – in fact, during January, it was hard to find anyone at work. Dad had explored the possibility of setting up on his own, but it seemed that most people were on holidays. Ominously, when he rang the Brisbane CIB number he'd been given, there was no answer.

Towards the end of January, we had to do something about enrolling in school, which was another kind of problem. Since we'd taken a new name, and had left Britain in something of a hurry, we didn't have any documentation. Nor did we have permanent residency status – that was still being worked out somewhere in Canberra. When it came time to enrol in school, all we could produce were temporary visas. In the end, we were enrolled all right, me in Year 11 and Nicola in Year 9, but we'd only be allowed to stay at school for twelve weeks, and to make matters worse, we had to pay fees.

'That can't be right,' Dad protested, but when he went to the Education Department, he couldn't make things any better. There was nothing for it but to pay the fees, buy the uniforms, and get ready for our first day in an Australian state school.

Mr Gorgon back in Manchester, see the problems you're causing us?

The night before we were to start on the business of enrolling, Dad received a late-night phone call from Manchester CID. The trial, for which he was to be a

131

witness, was now scheduled for the end of February. In due course they would advise him of travel details and procedures for his personal safety.

'It'll be cold, Dad,' Nicola reminded him.

'And other things,' Dad agreed. We knew what he meant. Up to that point, we'd all been pretty cheerful, feeling secure in our remoteness from Manchester, but the phone call had had a sobering effect.

8

The brown paper carrier bag on our front doormat was folded over at the top, and contained something about the length and breadth of a shoebox, but only half as deep. The paper of the carrier bag appeared old and crumpled, as if it had been used before.

We'd been out and about on some family affair – Dad and Mum seemed to make it their business to ensure we didn't vegetate at home, even to the extent of taking us to events and shows that were not their style, movies for example. It was almost four o'clock when we got home. Mum was driving our new car, carefully negotiating it down the narrow driveway and under the shed sort of affair at the side of the house. A carport, Dad called it.

Nicola and I, who'd been sitting in the back, grabbed the front door keys and made a beeline for the house, giggling as we ran. There was only one mango iceblock in the deep freeze, so it was a case of whoever was there first. But then came the parcel.

We both dashed up the four steps to the verandah and almost stepped on it, because the paper was about the same colour as the doormat. Nicola actually stood teetering over the thing, trying to maintain her balance.

Think of receiving a parcel – that sense of anticipation, the excitement and so on. Who sent it? Who is it for? You feel its weight and listen to the noise it makes when you give it a shake. If it's tied with string, should you undo the knots or just cut? But with this one, there wasn't the sense of wonder that you'd get from an innocent parcel. Instantly our situation came rushing back to us. We both knew what this thing wrapped in a carrier bag could mean, so we froze. This was serious.

Dad and Mum found us when they came from the carport to the front door. By then we'd backed away from the verandah, and stood out in the sunshine, looking at what lay on our doormat.

'Dad, Mum, there's a parcel,' we both said. Such simple words, but what an effect.

'Oh, God,' Mum said. Dad sort of slumped.

'Come on.' He spun us around. 'Out front. Away from here.' We went to the patch of grass outside the front gate. Dad took out his mobile phone, and dialled one of the emergency numbers that he'd fed into its menu.

Since we'd look silly and conspicuous standing outside our own house, Dad suggested we get in the car and go somewhere.

'Good thinking,' Nicola agreed. 'If that thing went bang, we'd lose the car too.' We hurried back to the car and took off. This time Dad drove. Every hundred metres or so Mum just shook her head and sighed.

Fifteen minutes later, we were in the shopping centre

coffee shop, waiting for a plain-clothes policeman to meet us. When he arrived he flashed his ID, told us his name was Trevor, casually ordered a cappuccino, and sat with us. Trevor looked too young to be a policeman. He wasn't very tall either. He had red hair, and freckles on his face and arms, and wore slacks and an open-necked blue shirt.

'What's it like, this parcel?' He idly stirred the froth on his cappuccino.

'Ordinary.' Dad showed its size with his hands.

'You weren't expecting anything?'

'No,' Dad answered. 'We don't have things delivered.'

'Okay, so we treat this one as suspicious,' Trevor agreed. 'It'll take a bit of time. Given your situation, we don't want to go charging in with the full bomb squad, alerting the neighbours.' Trevor was right. If the army mounted a full-scale bomb defusing exercise, everyone in the street would have something to talk about. Especially if they had to be evacuated. What sort of people are they who've just moved in? they might wonder. Trevor sipped his coffee, and seemed to make up his mind. 'You folks stay here. First off we'll send in a sniffer dog – '

'Poor dog,' Nicola said, but Trevor winked at her.

'Haven't lost one yet,' he gulped his coffee down. 'It'll take time, the handler's got to get into civvies. So hang around here, I'll be back. Let you know what's what.' In seconds, Trevor was lost in the crowded shopping centre. Mum and Dad ordered more coffee while we waited.

It was after five o'clock before Trevor returned, and

this time he carried our suspicious parcel under his arm. It had obviously been disturbed.

'You got a neighbour?' he began.

'Mrs Stone, yes,' Dad said.

'Then it was all her doing.' Trevor put the parcel on our table, then opened it and pulled out a flat metal tin which once had held biscuits. 'Family Assortment,' it said on the lid, with a picture of a parrot eating a biscuit. Trevor opened the lid.

'Lamingtons?' Dad seemed to recognise the brown squares with a dusting of coconut on them. Trevor, who'd kept a straight face up to now, suddenly grinned.

'Yeah. Our handler had just opened the parcel and was scoffing one of them when Mrs Stone came on the scene. Old dear on a bike?'

'Yes, that's her.' Dad nodded.

'She was pretty good about it,' Trevor went on. 'Very understanding.'

'The dog man ate one of our lamingtons?' Nicola couldn't seem to believe it.

'Two actually.' Trevor confessed. 'Gave one to the dog.'

'But they might have been poisoned,' Nicola said.

'Oh, the scientific squad handles poisoning,' Trevor spoke cheerfully. 'We only work on bombs.' He got up from the table. 'Anyway, it's just as well you called us out. Don't feel silly about it. Better safe than sorry, eh?'

After he'd gone, we sat for another two minutes, staring at Mrs Stone's non-exploding lamingtons. Then

136

Nicola took one from the tin and delicately nibbled the edge. I followed her example.

'M-mm, nice,' we decided. They were soft, with a chocolaty taste and sponge cake inside. But then a waitress who'd been hovering nearby came to our table.

'Excuse me.' She was about my age and spoke with a note of triumph in her voice. 'You're not allowed to eat your own food here.' Furtively, we put our nibbled lamingtons back into the tin and gave her a watery smile.

'I really needed her to tell us off,' Nicola complained, as we went back to the car park. 'She just topped off a wonderful afternoon.' Maybe we all felt the way Nicola did – small, a bit silly, and unable to look each other in the eye. Things like that never happen to ordinary families.

But we'd been ordinary. Once.

Since Mrs Stone was now involved in our bomb scare, she visited us later, which was an embarrassment we let Dad and Mum face on their own. As Nicola and I hid in my bedroom, we could hear Mum, Dad and Mrs Stone on the front verandah. We wondered what excuse our parents would make, and what Mrs Stone would say. Nicola went first, imitating Mrs Stone's way of speaking.

'Apart from the bomb scare, Don, did you enjoy the lamingtons?'

'Do you do that with all your presents?' was my suggestion.

'One good turn deserves the bomb squad,' Nicola

came back. Maybe it was sheer relief, but we both giggled as our suggestions grew sillier. But eventually, we became sober.

'Poor Mum and Dad,' I said. 'We're giggling our heads off and they're out front mending fences.'

'Come on, Em.' Nicola stood up. 'We'd better go and give some moral support.' But when we went to the front verandah, Mrs Stone sat with a bleak look on her face.

'You poor things,' she said. 'I've just been hearing all about it.' We looked at Mum and Dad. Dad shrugged.

'The cat was out of the bag anyway, girls.'

'I had no idea things were that bad,' Mrs Stone went on.

'We just had to be sure,' Mum explained. 'There's a list of precautions – '

'But calling out the bomb squad?' She shook her head in disbelief. 'These people must be mongrels.'

'There's big money at stake,' Dad explained. 'And the man's freedom, if things go against him.'

'*When* things go against him,' Mum added. Then, in a whisper, she repeated the key word. 'When.' Dad just nodded and smiled. An awkward pause followed.

'The lamingtons are very nice,' I ventured.

'Apart from us thinking they'd go bang,' Nicola added gravely. I could have kicked her for being so insensitive, but her remark made Mrs Stone smile. Then Mum grinned, and before long we were all laughing.

'Oh, I'd love to tell this story to the girls down at the bowling club,' Mrs Stone started to say, but Dad opened his mouth and held up one finger. Mrs Stone had already reached the same conclusion. 'But I won't, depend on it.'

'Maybe one day,' Dad said.

'If we ever see the end of it.' Mum was serious again.

'You'll have to give evidence, Don?' Mrs Stone asked.

'Some time,' Dad agreed. 'Back in Manchester.'

'You shouldn't have to go all that way to court.' Mrs Stone made her statement sound like a question. 'These days, they can give evidence on video, can't they?'

'M-mm,' Dad was doubtful.

'There was a case the other day. A witness was too sick so they got a video camera – '

'It's an idea,' Mum said. 'After all, our man's a menace, really dangerous.'

'I wonder.' Dad scratched his chin. 'It's worth a try.'

So Mrs Stone's tin of lamingtons gave us a sharp fright, a good laugh and some hope. They didn't taste too bad either.

The rest of January passed without incident – in a sense it was like a family holiday. We'd all grown more used to the house, but as it was, we spent little time there. We preferred to explore the city, which had a shady mall with pigeons, just like ours at home. We'd also go driving in the car, enjoying its air-conditioning.

We did trips to the mountains, to Binna Burra then down the coast to Surfers Paradise, which I'd heard

about from Dad. The place was a strange mix of unbe-
lievable sophistication and down-to-earth ordinariness –
huge luxurious hotels and apartment blocks crowded the
beachfront, throwing long shadows on the sand. Just
occasionally, like some kind of urchin, there would be a
small family-style corner shop, selling everything from
newspapers to fishing hooks and bait. On the streets you
might see an open-topped Rolls-Royce, or a huge white
stretch limousine, easing along the highway with its
windows dark-tinted, giving it a superior yet sinister air.
It was like a car with dark sunglasses.

'Bet the Gorgon's got one like that,' Nicola
commented.

Then we'd see a couple of kids our age, showing lots
of tanned skin, casually pedalling a side-by-side bicycle
contraption as they ate ice-creams or a young Japanese
honeymoon couple who'd rented a colourful Mini-
Moke for the day. We watched them stop at an inter-
section. When the traffic lights turned green, the driver
hesitated, not knowing which way to go, but the man
in the car behind sat waiting patiently until the Japanese
husband made up his mind which direction he wanted.
It was all so unbelievably casual.

Dad was excited. It had been years since he'd visited
the place. Mum had to order him to keep his eyes front
when we passed girls in the street who were dressed only
in bikinis, sunglasses and those never-ending tans.

It was such a change from Manchester – the whole
Australian experience was, but Surfers Paradise was just
incredible. It made me sad too, because there was no

point buying postcards. In a coffee shop we saw other people writing them, talking to each other about what they would say, or laughing together at something they'd written. Nicola and I just looked, then looked away. Mum must have read our minds, because she gave my hand a squeeze.

'One day,' she said.

Mum and Dad took shelter under a beach umbrella they had bought in Brisbane, while Nicola and I went for a swim – which is when the whole casual, easygoing edifice crumbled down.

The surf was something else. I had experienced artificial surf before, when we went out for a drive in Daimler, to Morecambe, or it might have been Blackburn. They called it a 'wild water wave ride' or 'the roughest Bondi waves in the North of England'. But those were indoor waves, made by pumps. In Surfers Paradise, they came by courtesy of Mother Nature, all the way from the other side of the Pacific Ocean.

For a time we frolicked in the surf, being knocked this way and that, until a few metres along from us, a small boy gave a sudden scream of pain, and fell over in the shallows, rubbing at his leg. His parents were nearby and they rushed to the boy's aid, but he kept screaming, and before long a crowd gathered.

One of the lifesavers came with a bag. I could no longer see the boy, because of the people who surrounded him, but his cries continued. Then someone sounded a klaxon and people began leaving the water. There were Japanese swimmers, who looked puzzled, but one or two Australians sort of shepherded them out of the water and on to the beach. Nicola and I went too, while the lifesavers launched a rubber boat with a motor, and began bouncing their way towards some swimmers who'd gone out pretty far.

'What is it?' I asked a girl.

'Bluebottles,' she answered, then, obviously detecting my accent, added 'you English?'

'Yes.'

'Well, they're not big flies,' she said. 'They're jelly-fish. They've got long tentacles that sting.' She went off up the beach, leaving Nicola and me at the water's edge.

The boy's cries had subsided, so we went to join Mum and Dad, who were sitting up, concerned at what had happened.

Later, we saw some of the bluebottles washed up on the beach, and Nicola told us they were also called Por-tuguese Man-of-War. They were innocent-looking crea-tures, resembling a handful of clear jelly, with a tinge of blue. They used their body like a sail, while their ten-tacles trailed underneath.

I shivered. With such hidden dangers, our casual fun day had gone cold. Shortly afterwards the swimmers were all back in the water, as if nothing had happened. We didn't join them.

Jellyfish weren't the only things that stung. Two days of agony followed. I was unable to bear even a cool shower on my skin. In addition, Mum's soothing lotion seemed to sting, as did her motherly words of so-called comfort.

'Well, you would go poncing about in your weeny bikini.'

'I wasn't poncing.'

'I know poncing when I see it.'

'Huh. Mother, that hurts.'

Some boys had been playing volleyball, and I just happened to watch for a while. Nothing wrong with that, was there? Ouch!

As it did back in wintry Stoke-on-Trent, school sort of sneaked up on us. First they had a bank holiday for Australia Day – a public holiday they called it – then it was time for school.

It was what they called a state school, one that was run by the government, and it was within walking distance. Naturally, the security problem brought us round the table for another discussion. Mum and Dad could escort us there and back – being preoccupied with the court appearance in Manchester, they hadn't bothered finding work in Brisbane. Dad went out most days, but never discussed what he did. I imagine he talked with the police prosecutor in Manchester, which he could do through the Brisbane CIB.

For a while, the plan was for us to be accompanied to school by one or other of our parents. We'd be fine when we were actually in school; the danger lay in the coming and going. But what were the likely dangers? It was a horrible thought for two innocent schoolgirls to carry with them, that someone might be after us.

As it turned out, we had plenty of company on the way to school. On the first morning, we dressed in our uniforms – bottle green skirts, a lighter green shirt, ankle socks and black shoes. Not much different from the uniform style back in Timperley but, we were told on enrolment, the school adhered strictly to its uniform policy.

'We have to glue them on?' Nicola asked, but she was only being cheerful.

We were waiting for Dad to back the car out when a small group of kids, dressed in uniforms like ours, walked along the pavement. Some of them were about our age, so maybe we'd even be in the same class.

As we opened the car doors, one of the girls made a remark to a smaller boy. They laughed, and as I stood with the door open, we made eye contact. It was one of those situations where we couldn't *not* talk.

'Look,' the girl said. 'School's only two streets away.' Dad was at the wheel. He hesitated.

'What do you think, Dad?' I asked. The girl paused, waiting for our decision. Dad summed up. Maybe we had the same thoughts. The danger – what kind of danger? Kidnapping? Not if we were in a crowd of other kids – too many witnesses. A sniper? He could get us in our own car anyway.

Imagine having to think like that!

'You girls might as well walk.' Dad kissed Nicola, then me, and we joined the girl and boy, then started off to our new school. The girl smiled as if she'd had a small triumph.

'I'm Emma,' I said. 'Emma Morton. This is Nicola.'

'Hi,' the girl said. 'I'm Jeni.' She spelled her name out for us. 'This is Thomas. My brother.'

'T-h-o-m-a-s,' Nicola spelled out.

I walked beside Jeni and we went to school. Jeni was smaller than me, dark-haired and vivacious. That's a Mum word. Mum liked to classify my girlfriends.

The school was, I suppose, pretty much like a high school anywhere, although this one was more light and airy than ours back in Timperley. Jeni was in Year 11, as I was, so we had already established something in common by the time we walked in the school gates. Thomas was a year younger than Nicola, so they'd not be in class together, but they seemed to get on all right.

Having Jeni to show us the ropes was a good thing. It meant we didn't have to do that pointless, gormless sort of hanging around, looking lost, that we'd done in the Stoke-on-Trent school. From our accents, Jeni knew right away that we were English, and she wanted to know more.

'Have you just arrived?'

'Before Christmas,' I told her.

'Whereabouts?'

'Outside Manchester,' I reported. 'Bury.' Jeni nodded. It didn't mean anything to her. But unlike dear, sad, lonely Christine, she had friends at the school. They arrived one by one, met with great excitement, then begin sharing details of what they'd done over the holidays. Much of it was about places they'd visited, and presents they'd received for Christmas – we'd do exactly the same in Timperley – and it was delivered in a way that excluded me, although they didn't mean to. In the space of two minutes, her friends called her 'Jen', 'Jen-Jen' and 'Jens'.

Oh, to be accepted like that.

It was as if they had a kind of language that I'd have to learn. All I could do was listen, but after a few minutes, Jeni remembered I was there.

'Oh, this is Emma. She's English.'

'Hi, Emma.' The other girls told me their names, and that was it. I was one of them – as easy as that. They went on with their conversation, including me this time – which was sort of generous.

Jeni began telling about an incident from her holidays. As she told it, she laughed a lot, using her hands and eyes expressively.

'Look, I was playing tennis one night, under the lights – '

'You? Tennis?'

'Yeah, I know. But *he* was there. He plays.'

'The things we do.'

'Anyway, his mother invited me. Very swish. Big house and everything. So I'm in my little tennis outfit – '

'Waw!'

'Skirt and everything, and we're all out at the tennis court. Little gazebo thing at the side, with Mummy, Daddy and him, of course.'

'Oh, him.'

'Sipping iced tea, and so I picked up a racquet, never played in my life, stepped out on the court going swish, swish, the way they do on TV – '

'Monica Seles – '

'Yeah, Monica Seles, when something comes at me, over the net. Whap, I go – ' Jeni started to laugh. 'I think it's a ball, see, so I look up, there's Mummy, Daddy and him too, all staring at me. It was a bat.'

'A bat?'

'Yeah, a baby bat. Fruit-bat.'

'Oh, no.'

'But that's not the worst. It got stuck on the racquet. Dead baby bat, stuck on my racquet, me trying to pretend it never happened, hiding the thing, trying to shake it off – '

'Oh no.'

'Oh yeah.'

'What did you do?'

'Started to cry.'

'That's awful.'

'Poor little bat.'

'No, poor little me.'

I stood listening to Jeni talk. At that moment, my feelings were mixed. I'd love to have written to Sandra, back home, to tell her about the unfortunate fruit-bat, although I'd need to explain what it was. On the other hand, *my* own story, if I could only tell it, would have made Sandra's eyes pop – my new friends too.

At assembly, the principal gave us a sort of ra-ra pep talk, a lot of it about how the sports teams were going to perform this year – words that sailed over me, with a few in-jokes that made everyone laugh, and caused a couple of boys to squirm with a mixture of embarrassment and delight. We were all exhorted to get behind the teams. Oh yes, Nicola and I would have to think about that and what it could mean – security wise – and the implications if we declined.

The first day in Year 11 was spent sorting ourselves out, moving from room to room, meeting the various teachers, finding out what the next two years would involve and how important a time it would be for us.

As far as the classwork was concerned, it seemed to be much at the same level as I was used to. Many things were different – history, for example, had an Australian slant – but English was still English, no matter what.

There were boys – my other half of the world's population – and some girls were pretty open about going steady with them. At morning recess and lunch they sometimes even held hands! My sister Nicola hadn't wasted any time in that direction either. Not only did she have Thomas claiming her as his own, she had teamed up with another two boys and a couple of girls.

It was very different from that freezing playground in Stoke-on-Trent, where we'd clung together for mutual support, with Christine making up our lonely little threesome.

That first morning, I found Nicola in the tuckshop queue.

'I see you've found a little friend,' I commented, with mock sisterly sweetness.

'Or two,' she agreed.

When we got home that afternoon it was obvious Dad and Mum had had a row, and equally obvious that it had been about us. Or more correctly, about us going off on our own to school.

'See,' Dad said. 'They're both home. Safe and sound.'

'Just the same,' Mum sniffed. 'If anything had happened – ' I rushed to Dad's defence, using cliches. There's safety in numbers, that sort of thing.

'Besides,' I added. 'It would look odd, big girls like us being dropped off and picked up.'

'There must be other girls who are met by their parents,' Mum countered.

'Yes, I suppose, and there's a school bus – '

'So there would be nothing outrageous about you being picked up?'

'It was all right, Mum,' Nicola spoke up from the fridge, where she'd taken out a carton of orange juice. 'Honestly. There are houses all the way and dozens of kids in the street. We walked home with Jeni and Thomas – '

'And others,' I said. 'Street's full of kids.' Mum just shrugged and turned away, and we left it at that.

If Nicola and I felt the pressure of the situation, well maybe Mum had it much worse than we did. The older you are, the more you can see over the horizon, the more you know about the awful possibilities that lie there. On top of that, Mum's loss of contact with her Timperley life seemed to be getting her down, and there was very little in the way of editing work available – most of the bigger publishers having their offices down south.

Nicola and I had always readied ourselves to embrace Australia – sure it was a shock to the system arriving at the worst time of the year, without preparation or proper clothes, but in these last six weeks, we'd made a good start. It was still hot, but now we were more comfortable in our house. We'd settled in, but poor Mum was just putting on a brave face. I could tell.

I changed into shorts and T-shirt, put my uniform into the washing machine, then went to the lounge to find Mum. Nicola was already there, talking animatedly about her day at school. They sat side by side on the sofa, Mum listening in a sombre, detached fashion, as if what Nicola said had nothing to do with her.

'So anyway,' Nicola continued. 'This Brad, Brad's the one who does Kung-fu, wants to be a Kung-fu specialist in the air force – but he only said that to impress me – anyway, he said, "Turkey's the capital of Istanbul".' Mum's expression changed briefly as Nicola went on, 'Teacher sort of twirled her finger like she was stirring tea and said, "Other way around, Brad." And do you know what he did?' Mum shook her head slightly. 'He turned around and faced the back of the room, then said, "Turkey's the capital of Istanbul".'

Nicola sat hugging one knee, with a huge, wide, gleeful smile on her face. Mum too had started smiling, so I went to her.

'I had a good day too, Mum.'

'Yes.' She nodded.

'It's going to be all right,' Nicola said. 'We'll be okay.'

Mum held out her arms and sort of gathered us. We didn't say anything, but I felt then that we should have done this before, let our feelings out, told each other we were frightened, not only for ourselves, but for the Cassidys as a family.

Dad came into the lounge and saw us together. He dithered, as if he could never be part of us. Since Nicola and I had a free arm each, we held them out to Dad.

For a second or two he seemed to waver, then he came to the sofa, knelt on the floor, and allowed us to gather him into our circle.

'No show without Punch,' Nicola told him, but Dad didn't answer.

In the middle of that night, the telephone rang. We'd grown used to these calls. We knew it was Manchester CID, calling from wintry Boyer Street. The phone always gave five rings before the machine cut in. Then came the woman's voice: number, leave a message.

After the beep, we heard a voice.

'Inspector Greyson, Manchester CID – ' Then Dad was there, and the voice was cut off.

These calls were always unsettling. I would lie awake, as Nicola did, and Mum too of course. We'd wait for the noise of Dad putting the handset down, then Mum would get up.

I found them in the kitchen, at the table.

'Come on, Emma, you've got school tomorrow,' Dad said.

'It's already tomorrow,' I told him. 'So what's the good news?'

'I have to go to Manchester after all,' Dad answered. 'They rejected the video idea. The evidence I have is too complex.'

'Oh,' I said. It was a small 'oh'.

'The Gorgon's got a good lawyer,' Mum explained. 'Inspector Greyson claimed it would be too theatrical if your father was allowed to videotape his evidence. In the eyes of the jury it would disadvantage his client, make him seem like a villain – '

Nicola came into kitchen, screwing her eyes up against the light.

'But he is a villain,' she said.

'Yes, and what about us being disadvantaged?' I demanded.

'There's no proof that he's threatened us,' Dad explained. 'So the judges have ruled there's no reason why I shouldn't give my evidence *viva voce*.'

'That's Latin,' Mum went on. 'Means Dad's got to stand up in court and be questioned.'

'What a rotten system.' I slumped at the table.

'It's the only one we've got,' Dad said.

'Anus horribilis,' Nicola supplied a Latin expression of her own, and this time I didn't correct her.

9

As well as feeding the parrots and lorikeets, Nicola had taken to finding scraps of meat for a family of butcher-birds, a kingfisher-type bird with a lovely musical call, which they sometimes sing as a duet. We'd all noticed how bold these birds were. They often darted down to pick up broken and crushed insects when we were taking turns to cut the grass with the Victa lawn-mower. The birds would settle on a rock or tree stump, wait till we'd gone past, then pounce, sometimes perching really close to where we would walk.

Mowing was Dad's idea of equality of the sexes. Back in Timperley he'd never let us cut the grass because – or so he told us – the mower we had in those days was a piece of delicate, precision machinery. But here, in the Raglan Street house, there was an old green one. It made lots of smoke, but still worked well.

Since the butcherbirds were so fearless, Nicola got the idea of feeding them with scraps of raw meat she scrounged from the kitchen. Before long, she announced that one of the birds had actually taken the food from her fingers. She was thrilled with her discovery, and feeding Mr Podge, as she called the bird, became a morning ritual. Other butcherbirds came with Mr Podge, but he was the only one who'd ever venture close enough to take the food from Nicola's hand.

I didn't want to intrude on my sister's little ornithological enterprise, so I kept my distance, and let her have this triumph entirely to herself. After all, it would have been devastating for my ego to be rejected by a bird. Especially one called Mr Podge!

And the date for Dad's trip grew closer.

It was still supposed to be the end of February, but somehow we all put it to the back of our minds. Nicola and I walked to and from school regularly now, always waiting for Jeni and Thomas, or meeting up with other kids at the end of Raglan Street.

Then one morning Nicola came in, bubbling with another discovery she'd made. Mr Podge only had one eye.

'It's amazing,' she told us at the breakfast table. 'He's got a dark head, and his eye is dark, so I'd never really had a close look before and, sure enough, he's only got one eye.'

'He must have injured it somehow,' Mum remarked. 'Fighting, maybe. Defending his territory.'

'But he's the only one who takes food from my fingers,' Nicola went on. 'The others are too shy.' Then she became thoughtful. 'You know, I suppose that's why he does it, why he's so bold. He's not the same as the others so he's got to take more risks. He's disadvantaged.'

'Something like that,' Dad agreed. He was reading the *Australian*.

'Levelling the playing field,' Mum said. She dropped her eyes to her cup and lowered her voice. 'Making the score even. Wish we could do that.' Dad coughed and turned over a page of his newspaper. Nicola and I got up and went to school, where we had another uneventful day.

There was a Cambodian girl in my class. Her name was Mai. She and her family had become Australian citizens, but she'd been born in Phnom Penh. When she was only a year old, Mai's parents had escaped from Cambodia with some other people, maybe about twenty of them, in a small boat, and sailed it to Australia. I found out about this when we were asked to prepare a five-minute talk about ourselves, which was to be called *Here Is My Life*.

Fortunately, we had time to prepare our talk. With the assistance of Mum, Dad and Nicola, I concocted a mixture – some fact, and a bit of fantasy – or as Mum put it, embroidery. There were things I could say about our Timperley life, without being precise about where we lived. I could also talk about my friends, about school, about holidays and events, again without mentioning specific locations. We all felt it would be pretty safe.

I wrote out my talk and read it aloud to Mum and Dad. It received the parental seal of approval. Ten per cent for delivery, ninety per cent for lying.

'You could mention Barney,' Nicola said. 'And

Daimler.' But, since I'd already written the thing out, I didn't feel like adding to it.

The talks took place during an English lesson. Mai was chosen to start off. Hers was interesting. Some of it related to the boat trip, beginning with how her parents and the others had gathered secretly at a waterside rendezvous, all the time concerned that the person who'd taken their money might somehow cheat them. But it was all right, the boat was there. Meanwhile, Mai's mother was desperately worried that baby Mai might cry out.

'But I was a good baby,' Mai told us, and that brought a laugh. Their boat had a small, slow engine, and once away from the coast, the seas were high and many people became sick. On the voyage, they were attacked by pirates. The pirates robbed them, but before they could do any nasty stuff, as Mai called it, they were scared off by a Malaysian patrol boat. Eventually, after a lot of hardships, Mai's family ended up in Australia.

When she finished her talk I shuffled my own notes, but the teacher dropped a bombshell.

'Would anyone like to ask Mai a question?'

Help! No one prepared me for that! What if they asked me questions? They were bound to, after all the dodging and evasiveness that I'd used in the last couple of weeks. I'm afraid I didn't have ears for any of the questions the others asked Mai, except to note that they came thick and fast. Then it was my turn.

'As you know, my name is Emma Morton,' I began. 'I only came here last December, before Christmas, from

157

Northern England, with my family, of course.' And so I went on with my talk, skirting around the real facts, sticking to the topics I'd rehearsed, until the end.

'Good,' the teacher said. 'Questions anyone?' Hands shot up and it was left to me to choose. I chose Jeni. After all, she knew more about me than most.

'What made you pick Australia?'

'Dad's Australian,' I told her.

Then it was a boy's turn. 'Where did you live,' he had a half-smile on his face, 'in Pommyland?'

'England,' the teacher corrected him automatically.

'Um – Bury,' I said.

The boy laughed. 'Sounds like a good place to die. You get it – Bury.' I favoured him with a smile. 'Did you have a boyfriend?' the same boy went on. But this time the teacher came to my aid.

'That one's a bit personal.' He frowned with his voice.

'What's your dad do?' a girl asked, but before I could answer, the boy chipped in with a jokey suggestion of his own.

'Bet he's a supergrass.' Others laughed at that. I shrugged and looked blank.

'What's that?' But I knew what the term meant. My legs were suddenly wilting, as if they were putty, and my face had flushed.

'Supergrass,' the boy repeated. 'You know, a guy who dobs in the IRA.' My ignorance had spoiled his joke – if you have to explain a joke, it fails.

'My Dad's not Irish,' I managed to say, but the teacher interrupted again.

'Come on, if you don't have any sensible questions then let's hear the next speaker.'

I have no idea who the next speaker was or what he or she said. I simply sat smouldering with – I don't know what. Shame? Loathing of the stupid situation I was in? Fear?

When I cooled down, I thought of Mai's talk. She'd started out her Australian life as a refugee, her family running away from whatever horrors or persecutions they'd left behind. But she could talk openly about it, gain sympathy even. I didn't *need* sympathy. I mean, who wants to spend their entire life cotton-woolled in compassion? To do that you'd have to *invite* sympathy – which means to let people know about your situation, which can sound like complaining. And I soon discovered that if you have an English background, you need to complain with caution.

I was in a group of people at school, talking generally, when I mentioned that I'd bought a CD on Saturday. Then, almost in the same breath, said I was amazed at the price. It was much more than we paid for CDs in Manchester.

'Books too,' I added. 'They're very expensive here.'

'There you go, whingeing again,' a boy said. Up to that point he hadn't taken part in the conversation.

'What?' I turned to him.

'Moaning, always moaning,' the boy went on. 'CDs, books.'

'I don't think – ' I began, but the boy was off again.

'You're a whingeing Pom. Nothing's ever right about this place – '

'Come off it!' It was my turn to attack, but he muttered something and went away.

Later than night, I told Mum and Dad what had happened.

'Oh no,' Dad said in mock anguish. 'My own daughter – a whingeing Pom?'

'Huh! I wasn't whingeing!'

'You were only having a good moan,' Mum added to the debate. Mum and Dad making light of the episode suddenly made me see how unimportant it had been. I laughed.

'So next time he calls me a whingeing Pom,' I said, 'I'll just give him the finger.'

'You'll do no such thing!' Mum almost exploded. 'The very idea!' But she struggled to conceal the smile on her face.

'What about a knee in the groin?' Nicola asked sweetly.

A day later, in the classroom, and outside in the schoolyard, I heard the expression buzzing around. Whingeing Pom. Then somebody else added the word Supergrass. At that moment I could have done without either of them!

Then it was Nicola's turn to blow things completely. It was her fascination with wildlife that got her in trouble.

Green tree frogs were a passion of hers – *Litoria caerulea,* as she sometimes called them, showing off.

Mr Podge had a formal title too, *Cracticus torquatus*, which Nicola used when she fed him and his family on Sundays. At school she had become involved with an environmental club, which studied threatened species and tried to save them. (But not us. Ha, ha, ha. Another of Nicola's jokes.)

This is where the green tree frog came in. There was talk in the newspapers, and on wildlife programs, that some of Australia's frogs were disappearing from the rainforests. This caused concern in environmental circles, so having green tree frogs at our place gave Nicola a seal of approval. Then, one day, she discovered an old metal bucket behind the shed in the back garden. The bucket had collected rainwater during one of the regular down-pours, and in that dark brownish water, Nicola found two of her tree frogs in some kind of mating ritual.

A short time later, she found the bucket half-full of frog spawn.

'Hundreds of them,' Nicola had said. Her eyes glowed with visions of becoming the toast of her environmental club when she turned up with this lot.

'Leave them where they are,' I said.

'Birds'll get them,' she protested.

'Surely not Mr Podge,' I teased her.

'Ha, ha, not funny,' she replied. So we had to find a container, transfer all this frog spawn to it, then somehow get it to school, where the glutinous mass ended up in a fishtank. The fish had been removed, of course. Then it was only a matter of waiting for tadpoles, after which the legs would sprout, tails drop off, and before you knew it you'd have scores of baby frogs, which the environmental club would release into the wild, having given the little green darlings a better start in life.

Meanwhile, Nicola's club went on a cane toad exterminating spree. Since this had to be done at night, it involved Mum and Dad – which gave us further cause for concern. The school year hadn't properly begun, but already we'd discovered there would be all sorts of excursions we'd be expected to attend. Both Nicola and I knew he'd be faced with residential camps later in the year.

Already Jeni had invited us to the movies, and to meet her in Queen Street Mall but, without trying to sound like Calvinist missionaries, we made lame excuses to put her off.

So we come to Nicola's calamity, which is all we could call it.

Somehow, a reporter from the *Courier-Mail* had found out about the green tree frog project, and she came to the school with a photographer. Since it had been Nicola's initiative, she did most of the talking to the reporter, and eventually featured in the photograph with other kids from the environmental club.

It was Mrs Stone who brought the newspaper in to Mum and Dad, and even she had a worried look on her face.

So when poor old Nicola came home that afternoon, Dad confronted her with the newspaper. Her photograph was on page five, and in the adjoining article we read that Nicola Morton, recently arrived in Brisbane from chilly England, had quickly fallen in love with our wildlife. The article was entitled *Frogs by the Dozen* and the photo showed Nicola delicately fishing a bit of weed out of the tank.

'Nicola, how could you do this?' Dad demanded. 'You know what's at stake.'

'I didn't think,' was all she could say. I mean, it was such an innocent thing. Maybe the other kids in the picture were already at home, cutting out their photo from the newspaper, showing it off, sticking it on the fridge door. But we could never have the luxury of being ordinary. 'I honestly didn't know he was taking pictures for the newspaper,' Nicola huffed.

'Don't reporters have to get permission to publish your photo?' I asked.

'That's pretty academic, Emma.' Dad spoke bitterly.

'Darling,' Mum said to Nicola. 'We must always keep a low profile, until – ' But Nicola cut her off.

'Mum, I know, and look, I'm sorry.' Her face had flushed angrily. 'I just want to be a normal schoolgirl, not having to think through every move I make. I mean, how long's this stupid thing going to last?' Nicola went off to her room and slammed the door. The walls shook.

Everyone else in the world was exhorting us to come join in the fun of life, while all the time we had to hold them off, and to make matters worse, we had to do it without *appearing* to do it.

'It's a sin to tell a lie,' Mum once said to me, when I was very young and had been caught out in some way.

'Even telling a fib?' I asked. 'Is that a sin?'

'Especially fibs,' Mum confirmed. 'Because fibs grow up to be lies.'

'What if I keep my fingers crossed?' I asked. But Mum just shook her head about that one. No fibs, no exceptions. Call them what you will, they were all sins.

And so we arrived in our new country, where every day was a lie, and we must tell falsehoods – because our lives depended on it.

Still, Nicola's mistake was one that none of us could have foreseen. When the photographer lined up his camera for the shot, what was Nicola to do? Was she suddenly to turn uncooperative and tell him, no, she'd rather not be photographed?

'But why?' the teacher would surely ask. Nicola would have to invent a reason.

'Um, my father said I wasn't to?'

'Why ever not, Nicola? There must be some reason.' The teacher would wait, while Nicola's face burned with shame. Everyone would be looking at her, their interest aroused by the teacher's questions.

Mum and Dad discussed the situation along those lines, and eventually Dad calmed down.

'All right,' he said. 'I'll go and talk. Tell her it's okay.' Minutes later, he was tapping gently at Nicola's bedroom door.

'What?' she answered, and I knew she was tearful.

'Nicola, I've come to grovel,' Dad said.

Still, the photo in the newspaper was worrying, especially in view of the one we'd received back in Illingworth. The one they'd stolen from our house. And look at the upheaval *that* had caused in our lives!

It wasn't until I was in bed that a further significance dawned on me. Again the night was hot and sleepless. The two photo episodes just wouldn't clear from my mind. Then I had a grave thought.

Gran's photos of the Raglan Street house – this house. They'd been in our album too, with Gran's captions on the back. I tried to remember some of the things she'd said. Was there anything she'd written that could have told him where we were?

I didn't think so. Maybe Gran had mentioned Raglan Street on the back of one of the photos. *Raglan Street is looking very lovely at this time of year*, something like that perhaps. But Raglan Street could be anywhere – any city, or a country town even. I reassured myself that for all anyone knew, the photo could have been taken any-where in the world – but in reality, there was little chance of that.

Perhaps he – the Gorgon who'd caused all our misery – perhaps he had no idea that we'd even left England. I began to relax, and let my mind run on to other things.

Then the phone rang. It was the usual hour for the CID phone call. My bedside clock said it was 0200. Dad let the machine take the call.

Once, during the day, it had rung with a message for me. It had been Jeni, calling to ask what answer I had given to a homework question. Simple enough – but again, it caused tension at home.

That time, I interrupted the answering machine and spoke to Jeni.

'Hi, it's me.'

'Emma, question seven. What'd you get?'

'Um – ' I told her my answer, but Dad was hovering nearby, and I knew why. Jeni and I talked briefly, then I made an excuse and hung up.

'Talk to you tomorrow, Jeni. Bye,' I said. Dad was waiting for me.

'How did she get our number, Emma?' His voice was cold.

'Dad, I don't know.' Someone had found another chink in the Cassidy-Morton armour. But in the morning, when we walked to school, Jeni made it plain how she'd been able to ring me at home.

'We've got one of these phones that flashes up any number that rings in,' she explained. 'On a little screen.'

'Oh, I see.'

'Yeah, you ring me and there's your number,' she went on. 'So I jotted it down.' A day or two before, with Mum's approval, I had telephoned Jeni to find out some information.

'Ah, mystery solved,' I said, and smiled as if it didn't matter.

'Who's the woman on the answering machine?' Jeni went on. 'Your mother?'

166

'Yes,' I said, without thinking.

'She's very young.' Jeni had an admiring sound in her voice. 'Sounds like a real groover.'

'Yes, a groover,' I agreed. We walked a few more paces in silence, then Jeni made another observation.

'I thought you said your mother was English. That woman's Australian.'

'Oh, *that* woman?' I thought in top gear, all the time kicking myself inwardly for being caught like this. 'Her voice was already on the answering machine when we got to the house. So we just left it on. We'll record our own message some time.'

Jeni seemed satisfied. But I wasn't.

What with all the newness in our lives, and the ugly threat which emanated from our old one, it didn't take much to send me plunging into a black mood. Some days school was positive and fun, I'd come home to find Mum distracted and withdrawn, with Dad moody and tense in the background. They both did their best to convince us that everything was all right. But there were times when their facade would crack, and Nicola and I would see the strain showing through the gaps.

At other times, such as the whingeing Pom slurs, I'd be down and depressed, and come home dreading to find Mum and Dad in a similar black mood – but somehow they'd have managed to pull all their cracks together, and they'd join forces to help me make light of my worries. So my feelings fluctuated.

One of the main sources of my emotional agitation was Mr Crombie, the teacher who took us for English. And it had nothing to do with any teenage crush on my side, or middle-aged infatuation on his. In fact it was the other way around – a kind of mutual aversion – and it was all my fault, which didn't make me feel any better. Nor did it cheer me that I'd fallen foul of the teacher who taught my favourite subject, and to make matters worse, there seemed to be no way of reversing the situation.

It came about in a simple manner, one of those times where you say something, then wish you hadn't. My choice of words made it look as if I questioned Mr Crombie's judgement, and all because of a term that he used.

He was giving out a list of novels and biographies that we'd study during the year.

'This year,' Mr Crombie announced, 'there are three texts which deal with the invasion of Australia – '

'The invasion?' I spoke aloud, cutting him off. He frowned in my direction then went on, his voice taking on a colder edge.

'The invasion, for Miss Morton's benefit, which took place on 26 January 1788 with the arrival of the First Fleet.' So that's what got us off to a bad start. Things could have been all right, except that I raised my eyebrows when I looked at the book list he'd given me. Mr Crombie went to the front of the room then turned to face me. 'You obviously don't believe there was an invasion?'

'It all depends on how you see it,' I said.

'From your – ' He paused slightly, then emphasised the word. ' – *English* perspective, how do *you* see it?'

'They came as settlers, didn't they?' I shrugged. Help! What have I got myself into? Only ten minutes in the country, and here I am arguing about its history. 'To set up a penal colony. They were colonists.'

'They came with soldiers and ammunition – '

'Yes, to guard the convicts and for protection – '

'They displaced the owners, killed them with their guns, infected them with their diseases and their Bible, destroyed their culture – '

'But surely,' I cut him off again.

'Yes?' By now Mr Crombie's eyes were blazing. What should I do? Should I say, I'm sorry for having an opinion? I apologise for questioning you? Instead, I called for help.

'What do others think?' I appealed to Jeni, but she just shook her head and rolled her eyes upwards.

'Yes?' Mr Crombie said again. I plunged on. I was becoming angry.

'Look, it was the way things were at the time. I mean, if it wasn't the British who came – '

'The English,' he corrected me.

'Yes, if it wasn't them, it would have been the French, the Dutch, the Portuguese, the Spanish – '

'*Olé,*' a boy said.

'They would still have invaded,' Mr Crombie snapped, with a note of triumph in his voice. 'Now, as I was saying before this – irruption – we will consider the invasion of

Australia through the texts I have marked.'

As I sat fuming, a boy hissed at me.

'Invader.'

The phone rang at its usual time, 0200, or midday in Britain. It went through the ritual five rings, followed by the recorded message. When Dad was satisfied it was Manchester CID, he picked up the receiver and cut off the answering machine.

He listened to the caller, saying 'M-mm' several times. Then, after what seemed like an hour – but it wasn't – he hung up. Since the telephone always woke us up, Dad assumed that we'd be alert and would want to know the news.

'Got to go to Manchester in ten days,' he announced from the hallway, where the telephone was. 'The court case has been brought forward.'

'Why?' Nicola demanded from her bed.

'His legal people wangled it,' Dad told her. 'They said their client's in ill health, wants to get this thing over and done with so he can have medical treatment, then a rest.'

'He can have a rest in jail,' I added my thoughts. 'A nice long one.'

'I think he means the Bahamas,' Dad spoke dryly.

'They know every trick in the book.' Mum's voice was bitter. 'They win every single time. They say jump and we do it.' Dad sighed then went back to bed. I heard them talking urgently, in low voices.

So we come to a bit of boy-girl stuff. I hadn't meant to go looking for someone. Not that I didn't want to, but it would have been an extra complication in my life that none of us needed – the idea of a boy who'd want dates and things, wow! Normally it would be 'yes please', but right now it had to be 'no thanks'. But still he came on.

He was the one who'd jokingly called Dad 'Supergrass', and now that he well and truly knew I was English, he tried to provoke me by criticising England, and he often succeeded.

'How'd you like coming to live in God's own country?' he began one day, as Nicola and I walked into school together. He came from the same direction as we did, so we'd often seen him in the morning.

'It's all right, I suppose,' I answered, keeping my voice offhand, which was a way of goading him. If I'd curled up and purred that it was truly wonderful being here, he'd probably have had nothing more to say. 'It has its moments,' I added.

Nicola rolled her eyes and left us.

'Has its moments?' His voice went up. 'It's not like Pommyland. When it's not snowing there, it's raining.'

'In season,' I agreed. 'But we do have sunshine, hot weather, and dry spells too.'

But arguing with him was like trying to capture flying dust. He changed to a new tack.

'We're beating you at cricket.'

'M-mm.' I nodded agreement, which took the wind out of his sails. Sure enough, he had nothing else to say on that subject. When I glanced at his face, he was sort of gnawing his lower lip and frowning. And still we walked together. I couldn't help smiling.

'What are you laughing at?' He was suddenly suspicious.

'I was smiling.'

'Why?'

'I was smiling at you. You're so desperate to prove how superior you are – '

'No I'm not.'

'God's own country,' I recited. 'You've got better climate, you beat us at cricket – '

'Yeah?'

'Excuse me,' I said. 'I want to talk to Mai over there.' I left him standing there, looking at me.

'If you don't like it here,' he called after me. 'Why'd you come in the first place?'

'I was brung,' I told him. 'And soon as I've growed up, I'm going home.'

'Huh!' he said.

Well, Romeo and Juliet had their problems too! But if I'd wanted to attract him, I'd gone the right way about it. It was as if I'd thrown him a hook. He now had a challenge – someone who apparently didn't like Australia – and it was his task to put that right. For the next two mornings, he made a point of meeting me at the school gates, but now his conversation was much less aggressive.

I really began to enjoy seeing him in the mornings but Nicola, bless my small sister, reported to Mum and Dad that I had a boyfriend. She was a bit premature, as at that point I didn't even know his name, but Mum didn't take the news well.

'It's all right, Mum,' I consoled her. 'We only talked a couple of times – '

'Five times,' Nicola corrected me.

I ignored her. ' – and he hasn't got hooves, horns or bad breath.'

'So, you've got that close?' Mum demanded.

'He's tall,' Nicola filled in the details. 'An Australian. He likes basketball and I think he's a vegetarian.'

'No, he's a Scorpio.' Coldly, I put her right. She knew more about him than I did.

'Oh, dear,' Mum said. On top of this, Dad was to fly to Manchester early the following week.

10

In the next two school days, our boy-girl 'relationship' developed further, but only to the extent of us finding more to argue about. His name was Greg, he told me when I asked. (It took the wind out of his sails that I didn't already know it.) I tried to convince Greg that not everything in England was as bleak as he wanted to paint it. He'd read an article in the weekend papers about homelessness and poverty in Britain, so he brought that up.

'All right, I agree,' I said. 'But – '

'So there you are then.'

'No, look,' I laughed. 'You only see things in black and white – '

'I'm not a racist.' He was quick to get that in.

'Greg, if you don't let me finish,' I lowered my voice, 'I shall strangle you. And how would that look on your tombstone, strangled by a Pommy sheila?' That brought him up sharply. His expression changed slowly from a deep, troubled frown to a huge, wide grin.

'I'd like that,' he said. 'Mind you, I'd put up a good fight. Take a whole week to die.'

Mai came to join us as I got into my stride.

'You don't see any shades of grey, Greg,' I said. 'For example, there could be some things in Britain that are just the teensiest bit all right.'

'Yes,' he agreed slowly.

'And maybe there are some things about Australia that are just the teensiest bit – ' I took a deep breath, ' – not so good.'

'Yes.' He thought for a bit, nodding as if with deep understanding. 'But they're all down south.'

'You rat!' I said, and Mai tackled him on the other side, until he had to pull away, laughing at his own joke.

Later in the day, Jeni buttonholed me in class.

'You're getting on okay with Greg, I see.'

'Oh, yes,' I answered airily.

'M-mm,' Jeni said. She packed a lot of meaning into that 'M-mm' of hers.

Sometimes I ached with longing for our Manchester days, Barney, Daimler and all the commonplaces of our life. The craving became especially fierce at those times when I'd been arguing pointlessly with Greg, or on the few occasions when I had time to sit at my desk and consider our family situation. I'd look around at the other people in the class, and think how different they were, how relaxed their life was compared to ours.

Greg seemed to think I should be grateful just for being here, and that I had no quality of life before coming to Brisbane. I learned to bite my tongue and not make any kind of comparison between what I found here and what I'd left behind, because as soon as I started to compare, someone would bring up my whingeing Pom reputation.

Somehow, I persisted in wanting to talk about my old life, using selected examples of course. The alternative was to base my conversations on the experience of the few weeks we'd spent in Brisbane, or else condemn myself to being a watcher and a listener – and I've never been that!

Luckily, I soon developed a strategy that allowed me to make comparisons. It came about in class. I'd made some comment about how we ate lunch in our Timperley school, where we had a proper dining room with tables, chairs and so on, whereas at this school, everyone just sat around or found a shady spot to eat. When it rained, kids crowded into one of the covered areas under the classrooms, where there weren't enough seats.

This caused a stirring of discontent. So we're not good enough for you? seemed to be the attitude. Funnily enough, Greg didn't join in, but even so I had to back-pedal furiously, saying that I really loved the informality of lunch times, and besides it didn't rain all that often. Even so, I got a few black looks. The damage had been done, but it was then that the strategy came to me.

I should have made my comparison by showing my English school in a bad light. I should have said – I really love lunch times here, it's like having a picnic every day. Then I should have said, in Manchester we had a stuffy, formal dining room.

I was so tickled by this new strategy that I began to think how I could apply it to some of the other comparisons I had made in the past – CD prices for example. Now there was a hard one. How do you make a virtue out of having to pay more for Australian CDs? Easy. You say, Gee, Australian rock stars must be really well paid, that's if CD prices are anything to go by.

But the next time me and my big mouth made a comparison, I forgot all about the new strategy and really blew things in a big way!

It had to do with newspapers, as we were doing a study of some of the local ones for a media assignment, measuring column inches, that sort of thing – and yes, Mr Crombie was the teacher.

The newspapers in Australia were one thing that even Dad complained about. The *Australian* was all right, he agreed, but he missed the ones we used to take at home, in what Nicola had started to call our PG days, or the pre-Gorgon era. During the week at home we'd have the *Guardian*, and on Sunday it would be the *Observer* or the *Sunday Times*, or maybe the *Sunday Telegraph*. Sundays, especially in winter, the four of us would settle down in the living room, each with our favourite bits of the papers, and we'd read until lunchtime. Afterwards, Dad would suggest a walk or an outing in Daimler and automatically, we'd all point to the window and the grey skies outside.

'Can't take Daimler out in the rain,' Nicola would say.

But once we found our feet in Brisbane, the Sunday papers absolutely filled us with dismay.

'Is that it?' I gazed at the fat wad of tabloid newsprint with little advertising fillers and fliers falling out – shoes, underwear, carpet cleaning. Every advertiser in Australia claimed our attention. The newspaper itself seemed to contain nothing but sensation, and sport. There was very little British news, apart from a lurid report about a murder that happened last year. We missed Manchester news terribly, both on television and in the papers, and when we complained about it to Dad, he was defensive.

'We didn't get much Australian news in Britain, did we?' he protested. 'Apart from odd spots.'

'We got Paul Keating fondling the Queen,' Nicola reminded him.

'He wasn't fondling her,' Dad said. 'He was showing her the way. And "fondling" is not a word a young lady should use.'

So in class, during media studies, I was rash enough to make a comparison between Australian and British Sunday newspapers, which caused a howl of protest – go back where you came from, that sort of thing. Mai came to my defence.

'Okay, it's really good here,' she told the class. 'It's peaceful, it's safe, my family have most things we could want. My parents love living here, but they still miss their old life in Phnom Penh, before Pol Pot came along. I often hear them talk about it. They long for the old Cambodia. You can't expect people to come here and forget ninety-nine per cent of their former lives. Pol Pot tried to do that with Year One and it didn't work.'

I gave her a look of gratitude. It was the least I could

do. Mind you, it's a good job I didn't get on to commercial television!

There was a happy postscript to this episode. When I told Dad what had happened in the media studies class, he laughed. But later, he came home with the airmail editions of the *Observer* and the *Sunday Times*. He'd bought them in a shop in the city.

We almost fell on him, but agreed to put the two papers away unopened until Sunday, when we'd try to recapture, in spirit, at least one of our Manchester days, although a week late.

Mr Crombie mellowed. I had handed in a couple of assignments which he quite liked, so we began to see each other's better side. When I mentioned it to Jeni, she had a different theory.

'He's had his bolts tightened.'

'Bolts?' I said. 'What bolts?'

'The ones through his neck. That's what everybody reckons. You know, it's like he goes in for an oil change every now and then.'

'Oh, I see.' I nodded as if Jeni's explanation made sense.

'It was a joke, Emma,' she had to assure me.

That was another thing I enjoyed – the different kind of slang and humour. Some of the expressions really made me laugh, such as when Jeni told me about a girl who'd broken up with her boyfriend because she found him dating someone else.

'So she dropped him like a schoolbag,' Jeni said bitterly. 'Wiped him like a dirty nose.' When I began to laugh, Jeni gave me a sour look. 'Look, it wasn't funny, Emma. She's heartbroken.'

Later I told Mum what Jeni had said, and was pleased when she smiled. It would have been wonderful if we could have shared more of these things together, but usually when Nicola and I got home from school there was some other preoccupation. Instead of us telling our parents things, it was the other way around.

On the Friday afternoon before Dad was due to fly to Manchester, Greg made his move. In a way I'd been half-expecting something like it, so had prepared a genuine-sounding excuse – but I absolutely hated myself. After all his patient testing of the waters and careful choosing of the right moment, I had to let him down.

'Basketball?' I said. 'Well, it's not my thing, Greg.' We were nearly at our front gate. Nicola had walked ahead with Thomas.

'It's not just the game,' Greg insisted. 'There's the crowd, the atmosphere and – '

'The thing is, my father's going to Manchester on Monday,' I explained. 'We're having a sort of family night – '

I waited to see how he'd take that.

'Fair enough.' He shrugged, and his face was flushed. Poor Greg. All that effort.

In the school library I'd found a book which had a single word on the cover – *Grief.* Seeing it like that was a revelation – that's what I was feeling. Everyone experiences grief, in different ways, but ours was especially acute, because we couldn't show it. We couldn't mourn.

The book said that if you have writing ability, you should use it to express your feelings about the one you have lost. It had been something I'd wanted to do for a while. I bought a new writing pad, Basildon Bond, and on Sunday night started writing a letter, putting down some of the feelings that I'd longed to express.

Dear Sandra,

As you can see, there's no address on this page, which isn't an unfriendly gesture on my part, it's just how things are right now. In fact, this is a very strange letter because I will never post it to you.

You may have wondered why I disappeared from your life – at least I hope you wondered, Sandra, it would be a blow to my self-esteem if my best friend hadn't missed me. Anyway, the real story is that we are in hiding from a powerful, 'branches everywhere' criminal, who has taken a violent dislike to my father.

Mum, Nicola and I adore my father and he loves us. We're so precious to him that we're out of favour with this criminal too, hence our need for a low profile.

There was more in my letter, and it took longer than an hour to compose, but suddenly, having written it, I felt much better.

On Monday, we rose very early and went about our usual morning routines. It was a very clear day, a bit cooler, and with a red tinge to the sky which made me quote the old rhyme:

'Red sky at morning,' I said. 'Shepherd's warning.'

'Oh heavens, Emma.' Mum cut me off. 'Enough of your gloomy prognostications!' Nicola came in from the back garden and washed her hands at the kitchen sink.

'Mr Podge wasn't there,' she announced with a sigh. 'The others were, but not Mr Podge.'

'Well, maybe he's off building a nest or something,' Mum said soothingly.

'They start nesting from July.' Nicola spoke as if this was a fact we should all have known. 'I bet something's happened to him.'

'Come on then, Nicola.' Mum gathered her cup and plate and took them to the sink. 'It's time you were off to school.' But still Nicola dawdled, as if she didn't want to go. Twice she got up from the table to check the back garden from the kitchen window, but Mr Podge had not shown his one-eyed face. Dad came in from the front of the house, and set out some papers on his end of the kitchen table.

'Of course it'll be freezing in Manchester,' he began.

'You forget about the cold.' He was preoccupied with his papers, sorting them into three different piles.

'Yes, dear,' Mum said automatically. 'You'll need to pack some warm clothes.'

We kissed our parents then went off to school. Which is when the abduction happened.

Jeni wasn't there to meet us that morning, but Thomas was his usual self and explained that his sister had something wrong with her stomach. The three of us walked on together. Nicola was unusually silent, still wrapped up with Mr Podge's absence. At the corner on the end of Raglan Street, Greg was waiting, lingering so we could go to school together, which was nice.

'Hi,' was all he said, then he walked along with us.

'How was basketball on Friday?' I asked.

'Great,' he said. 'Look, um – Emma.' He obviously wanted to say more, which made Nicola roll her eyes. I gave her a nod, indicating she should leave us on our own.

'Come on, Thomas,' she sighed. 'Four's a crowd.' Thomas looked blank, until Nicola urged him forward and whispered the reason. Thomas nodded, in a penny-drop fashion, and soon they were four or five metres ahead of us.

This time, I had decided to accept Greg's invitation, whatever it was. It meant a fight with Mum and Dad, but surely they'd have to acknowledge that sooner or later I'd want to go out with a boy. Nicola too, come to that.

183

The street was quiet enough, Nicola and Thomas were out of earshot, yet still Greg dithered. I was about to prompt him when a car drove past then, at the end of the road, did a U-turn and began to speed up, coming back towards us. As it drew level, the driver suddenly put the car into a really fast skid, which spun the vehicle right around, making a sort of 'schurr' noise with its tyres – before coming to a stop beside Nicola.

The front and rear passenger doors were already open and two men got out. Thomas stepped back from the kerb, leaving Nicola standing alone. I began to run towards the car, while Greg just stood, watching it all.

One of the men had already tossed a blanket over Nicola's head. Then a motorbike burred into the scene. I thought for a second that it was help coming. There were two men on it, but only the pillion passenger got off. The driver stayed astride the machine, keeping the motor running. The men bundled Nicola into the back. She didn't even kick, struggle or call out. Just as I reached the back door the men crowded in with her, and the pillion passenger from the motorbike, his face hidden by a tinted helmet, clutched me by the shoulder and spun me back across the pavement, causing me to stumble and crash painfully into a low garden wall. My books went everywhere.

The car sped off. The man who'd pushed me got on the back of the motorbike, which raced off in the other direction with a deep roar from its exhaust.

An old man, shocked and full of concern, came out from a house.

'My wife's calling the police,' he said. 'You all right?' I got to my feet. My shoulder was sore from where I'd hit the wall, and I was stunned by the suddenness of it all.

'Got to tell my father.'

'That was brazen,' the man went on. 'Broad daylight. Just like that. Bold as bloody brass.' Other people had come from their homes to see what the commotion was. Greg had recovered by this time, and walked shakily towards me, his mouth hanging open, eyes blinking.

'They got Nicola. Took her – '

'I've got to tell my father – ' I gasped.

'What was it?' a woman asked. 'Custody battle?'

'Better stay for the police,' the man urged. He tried to restrain me but I pushed him aside.

'No, my father has to know!' I started to run back to the house on Raglan Street.

That run back home – how many metres did I cover? How many minutes and seconds did it take? Someone with tape and stopwatch could tell, but I measured every step with a twist of guilt.

How stupid, I thought, how selfish! *I'd* done this to Nicola, not them. I'd set her up. After all the patient talk of safety, and my naive plea to be allowed to walk to school unescorted – there's safety in numbers, I remembered saying. But I had reduced the numbers.

Soon, I'd have to face Mum and Dad. So I ran as if desperately wanting to get there, but I dreaded the arrival. Already, from somewhere behind me, I heard a police siren.

Mrs Stone was out watering her shrubs when I came past, gasping for breath. Nobody runs like that without good reason, so she didn't waste time asking.

'Mum, Dad,' was all I needed to say when I got inside. Mum sort of folded. Dad closed his eyes and clenched his fists, before going to the phone. Then I slumped at the kitchen table just saying, 'Stupid, stupid,' over and over.

My parents didn't ask me who was stupid. They didn't need to.

Soon the house was full of uniformed police asking questions, of me in particular, since I'd been on the scene when it happened. I told them what I'd seen, then Dad drew them away, talking urgently with the senior man. At last they moved out of the kitchen, leaving Mum and me with a policewoman for company. In the background, I could hear Dad doing his best to explain the situation – to people who'd never heard of us.

'I had a feeling about this morning,' Mum whispered bleakly, gasping in short, urgent clusters of words. But she wasn't addressing me or the policewoman, she was thinking aloud. 'It was that red sky. I should have driven them to school. Right from the start I never should have let him talk me out of it. It doesn't pay to go against your feelings, not when they're telling you what to do, when they're so prophetic – '

'Mum, even if we'd stayed together,' I kept my head down, not willing to look at my mother. I wanted her to hear my excuses, to give me comfort. 'We couldn't have – '

'This was bound to happen,' Mum went on, in that same detached manner. 'Sooner or later something was going to happen – '

'We couldn't have made any difference,' I said. 'We might have delayed them – '

'No, you'd only have been harmed,' the policewoman spoke gently. 'You or your sister.'

'But she is harmed,' I almost cried. 'And I couldn't – '

'No, look, come on – what's your name?'

'Emma.'

'It's natural to feel guilty, Emma,' the policewoman said. 'But it's not your fault.' She was saying the right words, but I didn't want to hear them from her. If there's an antidote for guilt, my mother wasn't offering it to me. Nor was my father.

He came in from the front of the house.

'Whole street's thick with police cars,' he said to the room in general. 'Doors open, blue lights going like crazy.' The policewoman nodded as Dad went on. 'Why do they leave their lights flashing? They're not on the chase. I reckon they're enjoying the drama.'

'Something like that,' the policewoman admitted.

'All the neighbours are out on the street,' Dad went on. 'So how can we keep a low profile now?'

'Nicola.' Mum lifted her head. 'I suppose they'll want a photo.'

'I gave them the one that was in the *Courier-Mail*,' Dad said.

'Oh, that's a nice one.' Mum nodded agreement. 'Nicola was smiling, wasn't she? Our little girl.'

Dad had done something right – but I hadn't.

Two plain-clothes men came to the house later, Dad's special contacts, one from the federal police, the other from the Brisbane CIB. They were both alarmed, and at the same time rueful, that this should have happened. They had to spend valuable time convincing the uniformed police to let them take over the case and handle any negotiations with Nicola's abductors.

For a time, the two groups of police argued in our entrance hallway then, reluctantly, the uniformed officers withdrew. Our neighbours, who'd been spectators during all of this, went indoors again, and once more there was peace in Raglan Street. But not in our house.

The two policeman sat with us in the lounge. The one from Brisbane CIB did most of the talking.

'I suppose you know what happens next,' he said.

'We've seen enough television,' Dad agreed.

'I don't imagine we can expect a ransom note,' the policeman went on. 'But they might make contact, spell out their demands.'

'It's pretty bloody obvious the whole thing's designed to keep me here,' Dad said.

'Yes, you can't go to Manchester now. We've already let them know the situation.'

'The court case starts in a day or so – ' Dad started to say.

'Well, looks like he wins, eh?' the policeman said. 'Right now, we'll just have to wait and see. Hope they give us a call.'

Dad nodded, but Mum seemed not to have taken any of it in.

We waited all the afternoon and finally, the phone rang. Dad went to pick it up, but the federal plain-clothes man stopped him.

'Let the machine take it,' he advised. 'Maybe we'll get the voice on tape.' But the message was an electronic one, the kind of sentence you can create on a computer. It sounded almost friendly, this voice, jerking ludicrously on some words, putting stress in the wrong place.

'We have your daw-ter Ni-co-la. She is safe and well. Mister Cas-say-day, if you want to see her ah-gen you know what to do.'

Mum came from the lounge and made a dive for the handset. She snatched it up, but whoever it was had already hung up. We could hear the disconnect tone on the machine, but still Mum spoke.

'Give me my daughter, you creatures!'

The federal policeman gently took the handset from her and put it back on the rest.

'They've gone, Mrs Cassidy,' he said. Mum allowed a fluttering smile to touch her face.

'I see they've given us back our name.' She nodded.

'So have you, which is a start. Now all we want is the rest of our lives. Can you do something about that?'

'Come on, Lil.' Dad escorted Mum back into the living room. The two plain-clothes men joined us. They said it wouldn't be wise for us to move to another address, but they did promise twenty-four hour protection until things sorted themselves out.

That night there was to be no sleep for Dad or me. A doctor had arrived in the afternoon and prescribed a sedative for Mum, and promised to look in again in the morning. Mum slept in Nicola's bed. Dad phoned Manchester CID to explain our situation. He had to leave a message, as it was still only 0600 there and his regular contact officer had not come on duty yet.

We settled down in the kitchen, my father and I, to keep vigil, and what a desolate, cheerless business that was, to be helpless while somewhere – but in which direction? – someone was keeping my sister prisoner.

How was she, what was going through her mind, had they hurt her? As the hours ticked by, I wished for the gift of telepathy, I wished for power, for a keen intellect so I could solve the case – I felt so pathetically inadequate.

Poor Dad was also taking it badly. He sat, almost immobile, with his elbows resting on his knees, chin on his fists, staring at the floor. From time to time he'd get up and wordlessly pace out to Nicola's bedroom to check on Mum, then go to the telephone and stare at it, as if willing it to ring.

I had never told Nicola that I loved her. It's not something sisters do, and she'd never told me either, but at a time like this, it suddenly seemed an awful thing to have overlooked.

We had no appetite for food, but we had to go through the motions, so we sat at the kitchen table with a plate of uneaten sandwiches between us, and cold mugs of tea at our elbows.

'If Nicola's all right,' I said at last. 'And when she comes back, it's not going to be the end, is it, Dad?'

'No. Without me in Manchester for the trial, he'll beat the charges against him,' Dad agreed. 'But – ' He didn't finish and sat staring at his cold mug of tea.

In the very early hours of the morning, the phone did ring, taking us both by surprise. Dad hurried out to answer it, this time without letting the machine take the call. It was Manchester CID, I could tell that by listening to Dad repeat the information on Nicola's abduction. Then, for a while, he seemed to do more listening than talking, and when he returned to the kitchen his face was white and drawn.

'Dad?' I asked. He sat at his place and took a sip of tea.

'M-mm, this is cold. How about I make another pot of tea, Emma?'

'It's more bad news,' I said. 'Isn't it?'

'Leave it, Emma.' Dad collected our mugs and got up from the table. 'Not now.'

'Dad, tell me,' I pleaded with him. 'Since we've come

to Brisbane, we've done nothing but lie and evade the truth, but we've always lied to other people, never to each other.' Dad kept his back to me. Maybe that made it easier to talk, to say what his news was.

'You remember my partner Alec Cowan, from Manchester?' he began. 'He – um – went into hiding too, for his protection. And his family.'

'Did we ever meet him?' I asked. Dad seemed pleased to have my question as a diversion.

'About a year and a bit ago, yes. We had that barbecue.'

'I remember. He had a little boy and girl with him?'

'And his wife,' Dad agreed. Then he cleared his throat. 'Um – Alec's been found dead.' It had to be that, Alec had to be dead. It had to be something really awful to turn my father's face that drained-of-blood colour. 'Suspicious circumstances, of course,' Dad went on.

'But there's more, Dad, isn't there?' My father nodded.

'Manchester police think he – um – could have been – um – forced to tell what he knew –'

'What could he know?' I asked. 'Could he know about us?'

'They only say he appears to have been – um – ' Dad was delicately searching for words that would allow him to avoid saying one particular word – a word that had already dawned on me.

'You don't want to say it, do you, Dad?' I paused. 'The word's "tortured", isn't it?' Dad just nodded.

192

'Alec and I worked together,' he went on. 'Maybe we talked about each other's background. He certainly told me about his, so I suppose I told him things too.' He filled the jug with water and switched it on at the wall-socket. 'Just wish I'd known about this yesterday. You and Nicola would never have gone to school.'

Dad made more tea, and this time we drank it while it was hot. Then after an hour he got up and went into Nicola's room to see Mum. When he came back out he dropped something on the table beside his mug. It was the pair of valve cores that Nicola had tied together with a short length of red cotton.

'I remember them,' I said. 'Those hoons in the car – '

'I didn't know she'd kept them.' Dad flicked them gently back and forth with a finger.

We sat in that kitchen, cradling our fearful thoughts, until the sky became tinged with the red of another shepherd's warning day. Outside a bird called. Just a brief cheep at first. It became stronger and more assertive as the day opened, until it was a full-throated cry, soon joined by others.

'That'll be Mr Podge,' I said. 'Wanting his breakfast.'

'Then you'd better take him something.' Dad seemed to rally. 'Our girl would want that, wouldn't she?'

I took a plate of scraps from the fridge and, once I was outside, the butcherbirds came around. But they were wary of me and stayed in the tree above my head, making the special call they used when there was food to be had. Their beautiful bell-like notes echoed across the forest park behind the house on Raglan Street and, with the news from Manchester fresh in my mind, I wondered if my sister could hear them.

Or if she could hear anything.

11

Mum walked zombie-fashion from Nicola's bedroom and stood at the kitchen door, looking at us as if we were strangers. Dad went to her side and asked how she was feeling.

'How do you think?' she said. 'You're like one of those crass television reporters – someone's world has fallen in, so how do you feel?'

'Okay, Lil,' Dad tried again. 'It's going to be hard picking the right words – '

'There's no news, I suppose?'

'No – there's been nothing.' Dad caught my eye and made just the slightest shake of his head. So we had nothing new to tell Mum. Nothing that we'd *want* to tell her, especially not about the latest horrible developments in Manchester. She came right into the kitchen and started filling the electric jug at the sink. 'Here, let me do that, Lil.' Dad got up and joined her, taking over the routine of putting the jug on to boil. Mum sat at the table, where Dad had been.

'No news?' she repeated.

'No, I don't suppose they'll make contact again,'

Dad answered carefully. 'It's not as if they're after a ransom.' There was an awkward silence.

'Um – Mr Podge came back,' I said.

'You fed him?' Mum seemed anxious to know about the butcherbird. After all, he was associated with Nicola – he was Nicola's friend, her triumph and achievement – so he was significant. I could imagine that if the worst happened, if it got that bad and if we stayed on in this house, then Mr Podge, carrying all of the memories that he did, would become really important.

'He gobbled up everything,' I said. 'But he wouldn't take it from my hand, wouldn't come near me.' This was a Nicola-superiority that I was glad to offer to my mother, who just smiled and nodded. When Mum saw the valve cores, she picked them up by the red cotton and let them nestle in her palm.

'Nicola's right,' she decided. 'These would make good earrings. Gold-plated, they'd look lovely on her.' Again there was a silence, which Mum broke by gently placing the valve cores on the table and neatly arranging them side by side. 'What was it she said that day?' She looked up.

'Um – ' I began. 'She said something about one bad turn – '

'No.' Dad came from the sink to join us. 'She hated us always having to turn the other cheek.' He paused and lowered his voice. 'As I do.'

'Wouldn't you like to do something to that Gorgon in Manchester?' Mum quoted Nicola's words. It was as if she'd never forgotten them, as if she'd been keeping them on hand for a moment like this. 'That's what our girl said.' The jug began to whistle. Dad got up and switched it off.

'Something like that,' he agreed. Mum stood up suddenly, as if she'd made a decision.

'Then we'd better get you packed, Don. If you're to catch that flight to Manchester.'

The Brisbane police were more than a bit alarmed that Dad would come to such a decision, but he'd been thinking of it ever since he brought the valve cores out of Nicola's room and placed them on the kitchen table.

He told us that those two slender artefacts had seemed to accuse him, to demand that he take action. He was undecided – desperate to go, to make some kind of stand against the Gorgon, but at the same time had no idea how he could begin to raise the subject with us. But now, with Mum's blessing, it was different.

The federal plain-clothes man dropped in to say Dad's leaving would have to be done in secrecy. Since they had taken Nicola to persuade him not to go to England, it could be dangerous for her if Dad were seen to ignore their threat. The flight left on Wednesday morning, but there could be no seeing him off at the airport, nor could he leave the house in a taxi. There was a strong chance that Nicola's abductors would be watching for just such a move. After all, they must have watched us going to school every morning, working out the best place to make their move, and which one of us to grab. It gave me an eerie feeling, to have been the subject of such interest. And to know that even now, we were probably still being watched.

Cars that passed in the street, innocent-seeming passers-by, could all be there checking up on us, to make sure we did what we were supposed to do.

'We'll put our heads together,' the federal plain-clothes man went on. 'Find a way of getting you out of here unseen.'

But that turned out to be simple. Mrs Stone from next-door, who had come around early, offering her help and support, suggested how it could be done.

'Well,' she said, with her face full of innocence. 'I've got a blocked drain in my laundry.' The plain-clothes man looked at her as if she had suddenly changed the subject, without his permission.

'So?' he asked.

'I need to call the plumber,' Mrs Stone went on. She gave a very theatrical wink. 'And his mate.'

'Oh, do you now?' the plain-clothes man responded. 'What's his number, this plumber of yours?'

'Let me organise it,' Mrs Stone went on. 'I've known him for years. He'll be tickled pink.'

In abduction cases, it's usual for the parents to make a television appeal. In our case, the abductors had already stated their price, and we knew that no imploring would change their minds.

But, the night before Dad flew to Manchester, Mum decided that she and Dad should record such a message.

'Maybe Nicola will see us,' Mum argued. 'It might lift her spirits.'

But there was more to it than that. Mum and Dad's television appeal became part of the ruse that we'd set up. The videotape wasn't to go to air until Thursday, when we knew that Dad would be well and truly back in Manchester. It would put the Gorgon off his trail.

So the police brought a video camera to the house and recorded Mum and Dad's statement.

In the end, Dad's clothes for the journey left our house in dribs and drabs, taken away by a succession of policemen. After all, and given what had happened, police cars coming and going were quite normal in Raglan Street.

Early on Wednesday morning, Dad kissed us both goodbye, but seemed strangely reluctant to leave. Finally, it was Mum who urged him on his way.

'Just you go give him hell,' she whispered. 'And if his smart lawyer tries to tie you up in knots, just you tell him the Gorgon hasn't kidnapped *his* daughter. Let the jury know what kind of man he is.'

Dad nodded, then left the house, crept through the straggly fence, and into Mrs Stone's laundry. At a quarter to eight, the plumber and his mate arrived in their utility, got their gear out and carried it into the house, where they started work on Mrs Stone's drainage problem. It was a simple blockage, and by twenty past eight the plumber and his mate were all packed up, ready for their next job. From the front bedroom window, and safely behind our heavy net curtains, Mum and I watched the utility drive off. Inside was our husband and father, absurdly dressed as the plumber's mate. He looked the part, we conceded.

'Now we're thinking like criminals,' Mum said.

'Maybe that's what it takes,' I suggested.

Later, I found Mum in Nicola's bedroom again, arranging things on the dressing table, which she seemed to do endlessly.

'Where are Nicola's earrings?' she asked suddenly.

'You mean the valve things?' I said, and began searching. Then it dawned on me. 'Dad must have taken them with him.'

Mum sat quietly on Nicola's bed for a while, then smiled.

Nicola would be really pleased that Dad had taken her valve cores. When we were both younger, a million years ago in faraway Manchester, she'd begun reading about courtly love in medieval England – a time when infatuated knights desperately endeavoured to win some unattainable lady's favour, riding out armour-clad on their chargers to joust or to do battle, carrying with them some token of their lady's affection. Nicola was so caught up with the romanticism of it all that she'd started pining and languishing, sighing, and touching the back of her hand to her forehead.

'Uh-oh,' I said one morning, when she came wilting into the dining room for breakfast. 'Lady Penelope's gone and got herself unrequited again.'

'Oh, not another phase.' Dad folded his newspaper. 'Whatever happened to Save the Whales? With you girls it's a new bumper sticker every week.'

'Leave her be, Don,' Mum frowned.

Nicola took her seat with a seraphic smile. 'I forgive you all,' she said sweetly, sipped her orange juice, and reached for the Special K.

That night, Nicola came to my room. I was lying on top of my bed, trying to read one of our boring set texts. She stood at my door and told me about her new passion.

'Oh, wouldn't it have been dead romantic, Emma, just think, a handsome young knight, riding forth, carrying something of mine – '

'What,' I demanded uncharitably, 'one of your gumboots?'

'No, something more deeply intimate – '

'Your new Chipmunks record?' I turned a page, but Nicola ignored my insensitivity.

'No, a silk scarf, or a glove embroidered with roses and twining hearts. He'd pin it to his bosom and when he perished in mortal combat – defending my honour, of course – his steward would carry it to me, stained with my lover's precious blood.'

'Oh, yuk!' I said.

'You have not a shred of romance in you, Emma.' My sister put her nose in the air and left me to my reading. A week after that, she was into kite-flying. I smiled to myself when I remembered the incident. When next I saw her, I would remind her of it.

Surely I'd be able to do that?

Without Nicola, the hours were awful and empty. It wasn't so much not having her in the house; the awfulness came from knowing *why* she wasn't in the house. What was she thinking, what words did she speak, what could she see? Somehow, each whole day had to be filled in, which we attempted to do by keeping track of Dad's movements, in our minds at least.

'He might be taking off right now,' Mum said late on Wednesday morning. Then, in the early afternoon, 'He should be over Alice Springs by this time. I think that's the route his plane takes.' We found a digital clock and set it on UK time, so we could share Dad's day a little more, and be with him in spirit. It all helped to keep us from thinking about Nicola.

But when someone you love has been kidnapped, it's an enormous thought. It occupies every second of your waking life. You can't settle to anything – there is no task that displaces the knowledge that your sister is being held somewhere by someone.

You find something that you did *before* it happened – for example, a pair of shorts that I tossed into the laundry basket downstairs before going to school that morning. Oh, you think when you see them, I wish I could spin time back to the moment I put them there.

Mum stayed near me. She wasn't frightened for herself, but for me. We had a policeman and police-woman in the house, but they simply read, or offered to make us sandwiches or sympathetic cups of tea. We floated on tea!

I found Mum sitting on Nicola's bed again, arranging things on the dressing table, folding and re-folding the clothes in the drawers. I sat beside her. Mum left off what she was doing and put an arm around me.

'You know, if things go bad, with Nicola – ' she started to say.

'They won't.'

'If they go bad, then you'll have to be strong.'

'You too. And Dad.'

'Yes, all of us. But you'd be all we'd have left, Emma.'

'Mum, Nicola'll be all right. They only want Dad not to go to Manchester – '

'But maybe they'll soon know about that, won't they?'

'Yes, I suppose.'

There was a long pause, during which Mum just sat hugging me, and I put my arms around her.

'You'd have to be specially careful, Emma,' Mum went on. 'You know, not to take risks – '

'Mum, it won't come to that.'

'You're very precious, Emma. Y'see, I never said that to Nicola, before – '

'No.' Nor had I. My book about grief had said some-thing about this, about losing someone and not having had a chance to put things right between you.

'So I'm saying it now, Emma. And your father does too.'

'And I love you, Mum.' I paused. 'And Nicola.'

It would take a whole twenty-four hours for Dad's plane to get to Heathrow, then some more time to reach Manchester. The court case wouldn't start right away. There would have to be meetings with the police prosecutors, and all the time they'd need to keep secret the fact that Dad had arrived in Britain.

On Thursday, Mum and I watched the television news, which had the usual kind of introduction – police still have no lead in the abduction of fourteen-year-old schoolgirl Nicola Morton, and so on. Then came the message Mum and Dad had recorded.

'Nicola's parents recorded this plea to Nicola's abductors this afternoon,' the newsreader said. Then came Mum and Dad, sitting holding hands against a blue backcloth. It could have been filmed anywhere.

'Whoever's taken our daughter,' Dad began. 'I appeal to you to let her go.' Then it was Mum.

'And Nicola, if you're watching this, keep your spirits up. We love you.' Then Mum held up the valve cores and let them dangle by their red cotton.

'Well done, Mum,' I said, as the newsreader went on to another item.

There was a lot of media interest in Nicola's abduction, but somehow the police had managed to put a clamp on the reporting of certain things, and the showing of certain images, so we weren't pestered. No film crews camped at our front gate. This was amazing, considering the very public way the police had swarmed around our house when it first happened.

We watched the reports on television of course – all the conjecture, and the way they beat up the story with re-enactments and endless re-runs of interviews with the old man who'd been first on the scene. In fact, they interviewed anyone who had the least connection with Nicola, including the school principal, who said wise things about the need for safety these days.

The reporters were such a baying pack, I thought. Wouldn't it be wonderful if someone could channel their eagerness and have them do some good, instead of their endless clumping around, getting in the way.

At first no one had a photograph of Nicola, because the police wouldn't release one, then some enterprising reporter found the frog-spawn photo in the *Courier-Mail*. They had a field day with it – the photo was shown nationally, which caused some huffing and puffing from one of the current affairs programs. A lapse of journalistic ethics, they called it.

The TV stations who'd first run the picture defended its use, claiming that anyone could have found that photo. There was an editorial in the *Courier-Mail*, deploring this careless and slipshod abuse of journalistic powers. But Mum said they were only miffed because they'd had the photograph in their files all that time, and hadn't put two and two together.

Greg was interviewed, as was Thomas, but both had very little to say. To use an Australianism, I bet Jeni was spitting chips at missing out on all the excitement.

None of it helped to bring Nicola back.

Greg came to the house one afternoon when school had finished. He stood awkwardly on the verandah. I was reluctant to see him; after all, here was my guilty secret, come to remind me.

'Hi, Emma.'

'Hi.'

'This is a bit rotten, eh?'

'Yes.'

'No news?'

'No.'

'Look, I – ' he was lost. 'About when it happened. I got taken by surprise – '

'You couldn't have done anything,' I told him. 'It wasn't a time for heroes.'

'I still feel rotten though.' He stood awkwardly. 'And all that stuff I said, about Pommyland, I was only razzing you.'

'What, rattling my cage?'

'Yeah.' Again he paused, then a smile broke out. 'Mum's from Belfast and Dad's an Aussie, so we go on like that, you know, razzing each other. Taking sides.'

'It was fun,' I told him.

'Okay, just thought I'd come and see how you were. And your Mum and Dad?'

'They're both fine,' I said. 'We're all missing Nicola, of course. Still – ' I shrugged. 'I'd invite you in but, you know – '

'Yeah. Another time.'

Greg went away. I stood watching him walk along Raglan Street. Right then, I thought of poor, sad Christine back in Stoke-on-Trent, and of the woman and child who'd been in the street when our photograph was delivered through the mail slot.

I'd considered Christine as a suspect, as I did the woman. But what about Greg? Could he have had a part to play in this business – setting us up maybe, checking out our movements and reporting them to someone else? Could he have been sent here to make sure that Dad was where he was expected to be? Could he have told the television reporter where to find Nicola's photograph?

It's amazing how this sort of business heightens your suspicions of people.

The weekend came, and still no word of Nicola. We'd had one phone call from Dad, very brief, to ask about her, and to say that he was all right, but really busy getting ready for the court case. As far as he knew, the Gorgon and his legal people had no idea he was in the country.

Mum was fretting badly, closing in on herself. We

missed Nicola terribly, but from time to time we made cheer-up comments, which would seem to just come out of clear blue air. Mum would be doing something around the place, changing sheets on the bed for example, and I'd give her a hand, because time hung heavily.

'I just hope she's giving them hell,' Mum would say suddenly, and she'd punch the pillow into the pillow-case. 'And isn't Nicola the one to do it?'

'Yes, she can dish it out, Mum.'

I kept thinking of events in our lives together. It helped to laugh, because in a way I'd know that Nicola would laugh too – if we could only share these memo-ries. At home we used to read a magazine called *Girl*, until Dad put his foot down.

'There's a huge world out there, daughters,' he said. 'You should read newspapers, find out what's going on around you. Keep abreast of current affairs.'

'Yes, Dad,' we chorused mechanically. At about this time, Mum took me to buy my first bra. It was termi-nally embarrassing, especially when Nicola found out why we were going to the city.

'Your turn's coming, young lady.' Mum scolded her. So off we went in the tram to Arndale – our favourite city shopping centre – to one of the smaller shops, which Mum told me was ultra chic and exclusive, her way of sweetening the deal. We could meet Dad afterwards for coffee. In Mum's exclusive little shop a lady called a fitter came into the change cubicle with us but, fortunately, Nicola was made to stay outside.

When the fitting ordeal was almost over, there came a sudden scream from a cubicle, a couple along from us.

'Get out of here!' a woman's voice exclaimed. 'Get out of here, you rude girl! How dare you?' Mum popped her head out, and found it was Nicola who'd caused all the fuss.

'Sorry,' Nicola apologised. 'Look, I didn't know there was anyone in there.'

'Well, I'm in here,' the woman snapped.

'Nicola, come inside!' Mum spoke sternly. Nicola crowded into the change room with us.

'Don't *ever* buy me anything in pink,' she huffed.

'Nicola, just sit there. Count up to a hundred.' We were always counting up to a hundred in those days.

I had my back to Nicola. When I turned to reveal my new shape, she went 'Oooh' with her eyes. 'Dad will be pleased,' she crooned. 'Now Emma'll be able to keep abreast of the news.'

'Nicola!' Mum frowned another warning.

The fitter was still tugging my sweater into place. 'Oh, at this age they're such a handful,' she said. Nicola almost exploded with laughter, while I blushed puce with embarrassment. Mum grabbed Nicola and pushed her out of the cubicle. The poor fitter couldn't understand what all the fuss was. 'What'd I say? What'd I say?'

Later at home, when we'd gone about our own affairs, I overheard Mum telling Dad about the incident. His shoulders heaved with laughter.

It helped to remember my sister like that.

All over the world, Saturday evening is a bad time for news. But on this particular night, Mrs Stone came hurrying over to knock urgently at our front door. Mum answered.

'It's Don,' Mrs Stone gasped. 'On the television – '

'Oh no, what's happened? Is he – '

'No, he was on the ABC news. He's spoken out.'

At this point I came to the front door. As far as we could gather, Dad had somehow gone public in Manchester. Infuriatingly, Mrs Stone couldn't give details. She'd only been half listening, feeding her cat, when she realised it was Dad on the screen. We turned on our own TV, but the news item was over.

'They always give a summary at the end,' Mum said, so we fretted through the sports news and the weather. Finally, there was a brief reprise of the item.

'A Brisbane man on a witness protection program, whose daughter was abducted, has publicly challenged a Manchester man to a debate,' announced the news-reader. There was no picture of Dad.

'A debate?' Mum echoed the word. 'We've got to find out more. How? Let's think.'

We knew there would be news updates during the rest of Saturday night, but they were always sketchy, giving few details.

When Mum telephoned for details, the Brisbane police couldn't help, nor could we raise anyone in Manchester, and Dad of course, being in hiding, hadn't given us a contact number. So we fretted all weekend. Dad was doing something – we couldn't quite work out what, but something.

But a debate? It seemed so tame and civilised.

Endlessly we consulted the digital clock, checking the time in Britain. It was still only Saturday morning in Manchester – and what was going on? Ring, we said to the telephone each time we passed it. For heaven's sake ring.

We had to wait until Monday, by which time the item had gathered weekend momentum. It was in the Australian morning newspapers, and by lunchtime, it had been taken up again by television news. The long and short of it was that Dad had taken out a prominent yet innocent-seeming advertisement in the *Manchester Evening News,* in which he announced that he was back in town, sent fraternal greetings to his friend, then, for old time's sake, challenged him to publicly debate the issue that people should not take the law into their own hands.

Dad went on to suggest that his opponent should take the affirmative view in the debate. The ad, such an innocent-looking thing, had been readily accepted by the clerk. Anyone reading it would imagine it to be no more than some kind of private joke between two old business colleagues. But there were people in Manchester who instantly recognised it as something else. The press scrum got hold of it, and by mid-morning it was on radio bulletins. The Gorgon's lawyers suddenly found themselves being hounded for a statement. It was the first they knew of the advertisement, so they were caught on the wrong foot. They reacted immediately, saying their client was due to appear in court to answer certain charges, therefore he would not be engaging in any ridiculous public debate.

But the advertisement had done the damage. Why had it been placed? Dad was tracked down and interviewed. Once again, the Gorgon's lawyers were taken by surprise – the interview had gone to air, on television and radio, before they could try to stop it by legal means. There was talk of an injunction to prevent Dad speaking out any more, but he didn't need to. The chase was on.

British reporters, hot on the trail of a good story, began to pester the Gorgon for a comment, but he had barricaded himself in his office, so they turned again to his lawyers.

'Did you know that Mr Cassidy had returned to Manchester?' a reporter asked. The spokesperson for the law firm refused to answer.

'Did you know that Mr Cassidy's daughter has been abducted in Brisbane?' queried another. 'Is there any connection between your client's court case and that abduction?' Then the questions became more outrageous, which happens when reporters are safely in a pack.

'How do you feel about representing a man who threatens witnesses?'

'When is your client going to release the girl?'

'Does your client have a daughter?'

'Do you?'

'No comment,' the spokesperson sniffed. 'The entire matter is *sub judice*.'

Somehow the reporters found out about our Timperley house burning down, about us being forced to leave the country, and then about Alec Cowan having been found dead – Mum's eyes grew wide when she heard that item of information. It seemed there was no end to the connections they could make between certain events and this man who'd been challenged to an open debate – and these associations all became public knowledge.

The Gorgon's lawyers were forced to issue another statement, claiming that with all the media speculation that was now linked to their client, he could never hope to receive a fair trial.

By Monday evening the story had well and truly broken, and at last we could make some sense of it. Current affairs shows began discussing the difficulties faced by people who were on the witness protection scheme – their lives in ruins, living each day fearfully, while the criminals who'd brought it all about carried on with their respectable and comfortable middle-class existences.

Then, wonderfully, Dad phoned. We could tell by the grin in his voice that he was pleased with himself. Mind you, the Manchester CID weren't very happy with him – he had jeopardised their case against the Gorgon. In fact, there was a danger that Dad could be charged with contempt of court over what he'd done.

'Then go for it,' Dad had told them. 'Charge me. I'd love to have my day in court.' We talked to him about Nicola, which was the really sad part of it all. 'Wish I could be there,' he said.

On Tuesday night, Mum took a hand, showing her face on television to describe how we'd lived these last months, culminating with the information that Nicola was still missing. Suddenly, our story was open for public inspection. Next morning, the talkback radio shows were full of forthright condemnation for the kidnappers.

'Mongrels, ought to be strung up,' seemed to be the general opinion.

And in all this time, my father had done nothing but place an 'innocent' advertisement in an evening newspaper.

On Wednesday, two amazing things happened. The first was in Manchester, where a man telephoned a reporter at Granada television to say he had some information about the Gorgon, but he'd need immunity because he'd done some things – a bit of breaking-and-entering, arson, that sort of stuff. Then another man walked into CID Headquarters in Boyer Street, asking for protection for himself and his family. He too had things to say.

By the end of the day, no less than seven people had made their feelings known in this way. Dad was no longer the only witness against the Gorgon. Now he had company.

Then a man and a woman, out for an evening trail ride on the southern outskirts of Brisbane, saw a girl on the track. She was barefoot, delirious and running a high temperature.

It was Nicola.

12

Nicola was in hospital. That was the second piece of information Mum received when she opened the front door. The first was that Nicola was alive. It was the Brisbane CIB man who brought the news. Within minutes we were in his police car, heading for the hospital. He gave us more details as he drove, but his own information was sketchy.

'That husband of yours,' he said, by way of making conversation, 'he's doing a bit of first-grade stirring over there, eh?'

'Yes,' Mum agreed mechanically.

'There comes a time,' the CIB man went on, 'and maybe I shouldn't say this, but there comes a time when a bit of unorthodox action does the trick.'

'Yes.' Mum nodded.

'Not in every case, mind you.'

'No.'

Nicola lay in bed in a small room, unconscious now. She looked very flushed, with a waxy sheen of perspiration on her forehead, and she had already been hooked up to drips and monitors. Mum and I sat on either side of her, each holding one of Nicola's hands. A policewoman hovered by the door, ready to gather any information that Nicola could provide.

The joy of seeing Nicola again was spoiled by not being able to talk with her, to find out what she'd been through. We wanted to let her know that we were there, and that Dad was fighting back. All these things had to be put on hold, but at least we could be with her.

A doctor came into the room. Mum faced him.

'Don't ask me to go,' she said. 'I'm not leaving Nicola ever again – '

'No, no, Mrs Cassidy,' he said. 'You're fine where you are. It's a form of pneumonia – '

'How?' Mum asked.

'It's some kind of allergic reaction, we're not sure what exactly.'

'How is she going to be? I mean, her chances – '

'I'd say they found her just in time,' the doctor said. 'So we're treating her condition pretty aggressively. Normally, she might have tossed whatever it was, but in her situation, highly stressed, anxious, probably exhausted – I think she just lay down to it.'

'I want to ring my husband,' Mum said. 'He should know about this.'

'Yes, we'll fix you up with a phone.' He turned to the nurse. 'I think we could connect the loudspeaker phone down here, what do you say?'

'It's in the conference room,' she said. 'I'll get

someone to fetch it. It would be nice for Nicola to hear her father's voice.'

Magically, Dad was actually at Chester House, where Manchester CID Headquarters are situated. After a couple of preliminary delays, his voice filled the room.

'Don Cassidy here.'

'Don, it's me, Lil,' Mum said. 'Emma's here with me – '

'Hi Dad,' I called.

'And Nicola.' Mum sniffed back a tear. 'She's in hospital.'

'I got a flash from Brisbane CIB,' Dad said. 'I was hoping you'd call. How is my girl?' Mum filled Dad in on the details, telling as much as we knew. We both spoke together, running up a huge telephone bill as we learned, first-hand, the latest news from his part of the world.

The Gorgon had been arrested and was on remand. His lawyers had applied for bail, but the magistrate curtly refused.

'About time,' Mum said.

'The charges against him now are much more serious than the ones that involved me,' Dad told us. 'There are witnesses by the handful. I'm sending you a parcel of newspaper clippings so you can see for yourself.'

Dad would have to stay in England for some time. There was a mountain of things to be gone through, documents and the like – and it was freezing in Manchester, he added.

'Well, make sure you rug up,' Mum said.

'And Nicola, if you can hear me, get well, eh?' Dad's voice cracked.

'She'll do her best,' Mum answered. Then she pressed a button on the phone, and that was it. Nicola hadn't stirred.

Meanwhile, the police had concentrated their efforts to the south of the city, where Nicola had been discovered. Eventually they found the house where she'd been held. It was a farmhouse, isolated in the centre of a large field. It was deserted, of course, but there was evidence of its recent use.

The CIB man reported to us that they'd found Nicola's school clothes and bag in the farmhouse. More ominously, there was also a windowless room in which she'd evidently been held – there was a bed, table and bucket, together with other signs that she'd been there. When the police opened the door the room was hot and stuffy, and it was obvious that Nicola's abductors had tried to reduce the temperature and humidity with a portable air cooler, which was still humming away. It was one of those evaporative types, but all it did was to recirculate the room's fetid air.

'What's the betting that's where her pneumonia came from?' one of the policemen said. 'I reckon that thing must be chock-a-block with bacteria.'

'You're a medical man then?' his colleague teased him.

'No, I'm just a dad,' the policeman growled.

Nicola hovered, unconscious, for three days. Mum rarely stirred from her side, except for when I took a turn. The police offered their support, driving us back and forward, encouraging us to eat and so on. They also worked wonders, keeping the press away from us – although Nicola's release from her abductors was front-page news for a while. Then, on the morning of the third day, when I was alone with my sister, her hand moved. She pulled away from me and pointed to the ceiling.

'Look at all the colours,' she said in a voice that was filled with awe. 'They're so wonderful.' Her eyes stayed open for a few seconds, then she sighed and closed them again.

'Nicola,' I cried. 'Don't die! Don't die!' In a panic I reached for the bell, but the policewoman at the door had already heard Nicola speak, and in seconds a nurse hurried in. She worked calmly for a minute, checking pulse and breathing. At last she smiled.

'She's asleep now, so that's good, eh?'

'She's all right?'

'She's all right.'

I phoned Mum. Nicola had come back to us.

The next two days were a delicate, softly-softly affair. We were there when Nicola woke up. She didn't smile, although we did, tearfully. She lay silently for some time, seemingly bewildered, then frowned.

'I'm back then?'

'Yes,' Mum agreed. 'You're back.' She looked around

the room. 'In hospital. So, was it awful?' The police-woman came closer and smiled at Nicola too.

'Don't mind me listening in,' she said.

'Was it awful, Nicola?' Mum repeated her question.

'No, at first I thought my heart would burst from all the hammering it did, you know, when they grabbed me. Then they were – ' she paused. 'They were sort of very nice.'

'Very nice?' Mum's voice rose in disbelief. 'They held you for more than a week in that stinking room, they kidnapped you – '

'Well, apart from that,' Nicola conceded. 'But I gave them hell – '

'Good.' Mum hugged her again. 'I knew you would, Nicola. Tell me more.'

'I wasn't hurt or injured,' Nicola said. 'Or *interfered* with – '

'Apart from pneumonia. But go on.'

'Okay, it was really frightening at first, as we were driving away – '

'They didn't drug you or anything?'

'No, nothing like that. We changed cars, into a van sort of thing, and one of the men said, "Hang in there, girlie," and he sounded sort of nice – '

'Nice?' Mum snorted. We were getting her back too!

'Well, nice-ish. Because up to then, I'd been really scared, like, you know, vomiting scared, but I calmed down when he spoke like that. It was a sort of house they took me to. I've no idea where – '

'The police have already found the place.'

'I had to wait outside in the van until it got dark, then they took me into the house. It was hot in the van.'

'Did you see any of their faces?' The policewoman asked. 'I mean, can you describe them?'

'None of them showed their faces, except one who had a ginger beard and said I could call him "Ginger". We played Scrabble and I beat him – '

'What was he like, this Ginger?'

'A bit sort of thick. But he was kind. He brought me magazines and these stupid clothes because my uniform was – ' Nicola broke off and lay looking at the ceiling, biting her top lip.

'Yes, dear,' Mum prompted her, but Nicola didn't respond.

The nurse came in just then. She suggested we let things go for a while. Nicola nodded at that, so we settled around the bed and let her rest.

When we got home, Dad's pile of newspaper clippings had arrived in the mail. We spent a couple of hours poring over them, finding out everything that had happened in Manchester. Then a woman from the Juvenile Aid Bureau called in to discuss counselling for Nicola.

'She won't have to go somewhere?' Mum asked. 'I mean, to your place or – '

'No, we'll come here,' the woman said. 'When she's had time to settle back in.'

Nicola came home the following day. We had a grand ceremonial ringing of Dad, to let her talk, but after all the hours my sister had spent on the phone during her life, she was strangely shy with Dad, answering questions but not volunteering any information.

She had changed.

The Juvenile Aid Bureau counsellor came visiting. To me it seemed as if she and Nicola were just chatting amiably, but eventually Nicola began to open up and talk about her feelings.

Before long, Mum and I were also drawn into these sessions, and we realised that all three of us were feeling guilty about what had happened. I had already pushed my remorseful feelings to the back of my mind, and it surprised me that Mum should also have had a guilty conscience.

'With what was going on,' she said, 'with Don going to England and with the court case so close, things were coming to a head. We should have been specially watchful. I should never have let Nicola and Emma go to school.'

'It's understandable you should feel like that,' the woman agreed. 'We'd all love to turn the clock back, but they were ruthless, these men. If it hadn't been Nicola, it would have been Emma, or maybe even you or your husband.' She was good, the woman who counselled us, letting our talk run freely, then encouraging us to convince each other that there was nothing we could have done.

From Nicola we found out that one day in her hot

little room she'd begun to feel 'woozy', as she described it, then when she called out for Ginger, she found the door unlocked. The last thing she remembered was wandering about the house, calling for Ginger.

In the days that followed, a couple of detectives from the CIB turned up to interview Nicola, putting the kind of questions that we'd never have thought to ask. They also had her create an identikit picture of Ginger, and asked if she had noticed any tattoos or marks on his arms. How did he speak? What kind of accent did he have?

Apart from reasonable descriptions, Nicola gave them another clue. Ginger had a sister named Noelene.

'Did he tell you about her?' the detective asked.

'No, we were playing Scrabble and he put that down on the board,' Nicola answered. 'He was very pleased with himself for making such a long word, but I said that names weren't allowed – but he told me it was his sister's, so I let him have the points.'

The police thought it was a worthwhile germ of information, but there was nothing more Nicola could add. She'd had one chance of looking out of a window in the farmhouse, but there was only bush outside. Eventually, the detectives had all they could get out of her, so they turned to other matters.

In piecing the events together, the police worked out that the abductors had been willing to kidnap Nicola and hold her, but they were not inclined to go further than that. And so, with the news from Manchester, they must have realised that the Gorgon was almost finished, and decided to disappear. Whether they were aware that Nicola was coming down with pneumonia is something we'll never know.

In a way I hoped they'd never find them. If they did, it would mean a trial, with Nicola as a witness. Right then, that wasn't what any of us wanted. After a few days of questions and visits, the police stopped coming and we had Nicola to ourselves.

I wrote to Sandra. I got out my Basildon Bond and this time, I really wrote her a letter, telling all about what had happened to us. After all, she'd already know most of it through Dad's public utterances.

. . . So how are things at the old school, Sandra? How is Ms Sangster, and dear old Muddles? Such a lot has been happening to us, as you've probably heard.

Believe me, Sandra, I absolutely hated just having to leave like that, and then not being able to make contact with you and the others, that was horrible and wrenching too.

Do you still see that boy on the bus? You know the one I mean. I bet he's going steady with someone. Lucky her!

There are times I'd love to be there with you, as if none of this had ever happened. At other times I think I never want to see Manchester again, after all that happened there, and all that we've lost as a family. My address is at the top. I hope you can write.

Love from your friend,
Emma.

Of course I told Mum I had written the letter, and showed it to her with the stamp on, all ready to mail. At first she was doubtful.

'Emma, do you think you should?'

'Why not, Mum?' I said. 'It's over now. We're the Cassidys again and the Gorgon's done his dash. That's Australian slang.'

Mum sighed, then smiled.

'Well, why not?'

So I left the house unaccompanied and free, said g'day to Mrs Stone, who was watering her plants, then walked to the post office with my letter for Sandra.

We weren't fooling ourselves; we had been 'lucky' with Nicola's abductors and the way they'd behaved, especially in view of what happened to Dad's colleague in Manchester. More than once I lay awake in a cold sweat, as I thought of how things might have been.

'Nicola,' I called out to her one night.

'Yes,' she answered, from her bed in the next room.

'Nothing. Just making sure you're there.'

'Yep. I'm still here.'

That's what we'd come to. Nicola didn't think it odd that I should ask such a question in the middle of the night, and I didn't consider it unusual that my sister should be lying wide awake.

I padded into her room and pulled back the bed covers.

'Move over, Nicola.'

'This bed's very narrow.'

'It's big enough.' So we snuggled down together and I whispered into my sister's ear, 'I should never have let you out of my sight.'

Nicola gave just the slightest shake of her shoulder, which might have meant anything – a snort of sisterly amusement, or a sniff. Who knows? But we got some sleep.

We were eating dinner, watching television together. It was the seven o'clock news, the boring bit about financial stuff, the state of the Australian dollar and that sort of thing.

The newsreader announced, 'Less people were seeking work last month than – ' But whatever else he said was lost, because suddenly Nicola yelled at the screen.

'*Fewer* people! Can't you say *fewer*?' Then she thrust her plate aside and ran to her bedroom, slamming the door. We could hear her sobbing. Mum and I hurried to her.

'It's all right, darling.'

'Less people,' Nicola said, with scorn in her voice. 'Why can't they ever say fewer?' Of all the language differences Nicola had noted, this was the one that really bugged her.

'I'll write to them,' Mum promised. 'Put them right.'

'I was stupid,' Nicola said through her sobs. 'Honestly I was so stupid.' Mum and I looked at each other helplessly. We knew what she meant.

Each member of the Cassidy family had been damaged and bruised by the business with the Gorgon, but Nicola was going to be our lasting casualty.

Mr Podge, the butcherbird, still came around, and Nicola resumed feeding him. She was pleased that I'd kept up this morning routine, and doubly pleased when she learned that not once had he deigned to take the food scraps from my fingers.

'Emma, I'll show you how,' she said. 'See, keep your eyes down. If you stare at him, he'll never trust you.' So I tried that and sure enough, Mr Podge took the scrap of meat from my fingers.

In a way it was exciting, as if I'd suddenly been accepted.

In late April Dad returned to Raglan Street, amid great excitement. Mum had kept him pretty well informed about Nicola's abduction experience, so Dad skirted around that. Instead, he asked about us in general. He would tell a bit of his news, then we'd relate some of ours. Between our two bubbling founts of information, it took a long time to satisfy each other with the facts.

Dad had fresh news. It seemed the Gorgon was genuinely in ill-health. His world had suddenly collapsed about him, with no lawyer able to dig him out of the mess he was in – and, more significantly, no criminal connection willing to carry out his wishes.

The Gorgon was now powerless and pathetic, reduced to nothing. In fact, if he were to walk free, the chances were that he'd need protection himself. Such was the information he had about other people.

What had made it all the worse for him was the situation of his own daughter, who'd known nothing of the Gorgon's underworld connections. She was nineteen and had just started at the University of Manchester, but after my father made our plight public, and when the press speculation began to grow, she had gone into hiding.

When Dad told us that piece of news, I immediately felt sorry for her – giving up her friends, her hopes and ambitions.

'But what about us, Dad?' Nicola asked.

'I would say, my darling,' Dad said slowly. 'I would say that we can go where we please, do what we like – '

'It's over then?' Mum said. Dad gave her a wink.

As a funny little postscript, Nicola found her valve core earrings hanging beside her mirror, just as she had left them at the end of that day we all went to Mount Tamborine and met the hoons.

'Look what I found,' she said to Mum and me. 'Do you think I should ask Dad about them?'

'M-mm, maybe not,' Mum answered, and put the valve cores back where they'd been hanging. 'They served their purpose.'

We didn't have a family discussion about it, but each of us, in our own way, decided to stay at Raglan Street. It was autumn in Brisbane, with lovely clear blue-sky days, and a certain crispness in the air. The trees didn't shed their leaves the way they did back home, which I'd always miss – walking ankle deep in them, kicking them up, sniffing the air for the burning smell you get at that time of year. But the Brisbane autumn was lovely in its own way, and there was a winter to come.

We settled on another school, a private girls' school, so that was a bit like turning full circle. Somehow the idea of going back to our old school, with Jeni and Greg, didn't seem such a good one. We'd have to handle the questions all over again, and we'd be notorious when we just wanted to be ordinary. So, after only a brief flirtation, it was goodbye to the other fifty per cent of the population – although some of my new friends told me that we'd get to attend dances throughout the year, with boys.

I never saw Greg again. Somehow, having doubted him made it, well, impossible to even *want* to see him again, which is a shame as he was quite nice. Once that little finger of suspicion was raised, there would always be misgiving on my part.

See how this thing continues to do its damage?

Dad set up on his own in the city, and Mum found some freelance editing to do. We worked on the house and in the garden.

I'll never forget my Manchester days of course, none of us will ever do that. And I know it'll be easy enough to go back there to visit, or to stay and work if I want to. Maybe study there too, who knows? I keep thinking of those happy Australians I met on our flight out of England. Perhaps I could be like one of them – that girl who sat with the boy, for example.

Somehow, I forgot all about my letter to Sandra until a few weeks later, when Mum brought it up.

'Did she ever reply, Emma?'

'No,' I said. 'Maybe the letter went astray.'

'Or maybe she's moved.'

'Something like that,' I agreed.

Dad had his eye on an old Daimler. It wasn't the same model as Daimler, nor was it in such good condition.

'In fact it's a bit run down,' he said. 'But what do you think, girls?

'M-mm,' Mum said. 'We don't have a proper garage here.'

'It wouldn't be air-conditioned,' I countered. 'And think of all that work fixing it up.'

'No, Dad.' Nicola shook her head. 'It just wouldn't be Daimler. There wouldn't be any memories with it.'

'M-mm, yes, Perhaps you're right, Nicola,' Dad agreed.

'And besides, Emma and me are getting a bit old for that sort of thing.'

So that's where we left it.

About the story

Most kinds of writing, whether it's a novel, play or television script, start out from a very small idea. Often it's no more than a single word or phrase, which grows into a sentence, then a paragraph, before becoming a series of notes and jottings as the writer starts to develop characters and situations. In my case, the single word that inspired this novel was 'alienation'.

My lonely little word soon grew into a sentence along these lines: I'd like to examine how the teenage children of a family cope when they're faced with sudden alienation from their own background.

Such a story would require some kind of event in the teenagers' lives, to cause the alienation, so my idea was to have their father involved in a situation which upset people and made him an outcast – my first choice was to make him a 'whistleblower' who had exposed corruption in a large organisation. Because of their father's action, the children would be shunned and rejected at school and in other ways. How they coped with this, and what happened to them, would be the story.

Then, by coincidence, I came across an edition of the

British magazine, the *Spectator*, 26 March 1994, which contained an article by Alasdair Palmer entitled 'The Case of the Vanishing Witnesses'. Alasdair Palmer's article shows how people in Manchester and other parts of Britain have 'disappeared' – left their former lives, homes, friends, jobs and all of their connections to start an entirely new life elsewhere. People go into hiding in this way because they were innocent bystanders who witnessed a crime being committed. What they saw and heard becomes vital evidence for the police in their court case against the criminal. But people are often reluctant to give evidence, because of threats made against them or their family.

Faced with this problem, the police make a bargain with the witness: in return for his or her evidence in court, they will provide him or her with a new identity and relocate him or her to another part of the country. The police in Manchester have assisted in hundreds of these disappearances, which cost about £10 000 each, but are cheap in comparison with the expense of a collapsed prosecution, which in some cases may run to more than a million pounds.

Alasdair Palmer's article goes on to say that the children of relocated families often suffer badly when they are taken away from school, from friends, relatives and perhaps even a budding romantic relationship. So here was alienation on a big scale – with the possibility of an on-going threat to the family and a heightened need to be watchful and distrustful of strangers.

This was a more complete alienation and a witness

protection became the reason for my fictitious family's misfortune – the father had innocently become involved with a 'Mr Big', who had powerful friends. Now, with the subject matter settled, it was possible to look at some consequences of the father's role. Having brought this on his family, would he experience guilt? Would the other family members blame him in some way for their predicament? How would a family weather such a massive strain on their lives?

I liked the idea of starting the story in Manchester then moving the action to the other side of the world, to Australia, creating further alienation by having the family leave wintry England to arrive tired, jet-lagged and dispirited in steamy Brisbane, with its storms, marauding insects and disturbed nights caused by the enervating heat.

The Australian side of the story presented no problems for me since I lived in Brisbane, but if the Manchester side was to be accurate, it was clear to me I'd have to go there to check locations and meet a few people. So, in September 1994, with the novel still only in outline form, I went to Britain to gather some impressions and details that would be useful in the story. It soon became obvious that there is nothing quite like being on the scene with a note-book, video camera and tape recorder.

As part of this fact finding mission, I spoke with senior girls at Wright Robinson High School and at Brookside Girls' School in Manchester. They told me of their life-style and of their knowledge of Australia, both of which were to play a part in the novel. It was the girls who suggested that Knutsford would be an ideal location for my family's first night away from their home, and I duly paid this charming little town a visit.

I should add that as far as I'm aware, there is no Knutsford Inn – certainly not like the one I describe in the first two chapters.

But the most important element of the story was how relocated families actually fare once they settle into their new life and identity. Since very few witnesses ever come out of hiding to describe how they are coping, I had to resort to my imagination for this detail – how would a family cope with their isolation from relatives and from friends? How would parents handle the delicate task of explaining to younger family members the need to be careful? Would they have to invent a past? How do they learn to become evasive with well-meaning but overly curious neighbours? And what about the children's school records, together with a thousand other details that less troubled families would never have to consider?

Australia too has witness protection programs operating in most States, with as many as 400 people officially living in hiding at any one time. In an article by Janet Fife-Yeomans in the *Weekend Australian*, 26 February 1995, one protected witness who did speak out claimed that the police 'sit you down and tell you what it will mean and they certainly don't say it will be a bed of roses but you don't realise what it's like until you do it.'

This witness went on to describe being moved with

her two children to a flat in another State, with twenty-four hour police protection just across the road. She was unable to go anywhere without an escort, whose task it was to check out her flat every time they returned. Her children couldn't attend school for three months and as a result one of them suffered learning difficulties.

For this witness, things eventually quietened down, although she and her children can never relax their guard. The man she gave evidence against had the charges dropped, so he is now free to go where he pleases – but police believe he is both dangerous and vengeful.

My description of the police removal of the Cassidy household is pure invention – but shortly after the novel was finished, there came a real-life event in Sydney where the father of a family of four teenage children had given evidence against some people so, for their safety, the police removed the family to a place of protection.

An article by Ian Verrender in the *Sydney Morning Herald*, 24 June 1995, described the Sunday morning removal of the family's effects as 'a military style operation ... [where] ... police patrolled the streets and cordoned off the small suburban pocket ... [while] ... teams of removalists systematically went through the house and loaded its contents into vans.' By the time they finished in the late afternoon, 'all evidence of the family's existence had been erased. Even the family dog had disappeared.'

So, for some families, and their removal from the face of the earth, my description of such events may have been close enough to the truth after all.

On a more poignant note, Ian Verrender reported that all four of the children suffered losses in some way. The oldest son of the family had to give up a promising apprenticeship and walk away from his steady girlfriend, probably never to see her again. His sister, the eldest daughter of the family, had, after years of training and dedication, won a scholarship to one of the world's premier ballet schools, which would virtually have assured her of a career. But, because of her need to go into hiding, she was unable to take up the place.

None of the children who are involved in witness protection programs ever seem to be given any choice in what happens to them.

David McRobbie